T0146429

FACES OF DEATH

FACES OF DEATH

TALES OF THE MYSTERIOUS CURSE

MONTY

FACES OF DEATH
TALES OF THE MYSTERIOUS CURSE

iUniverse books may be ordered through booksellers or by contacting:

iUniverse
1663 Liberty Drive
Bloomington, IN 47403
www.iuniverse.com
1-800-Authors (1-800-288-4677)

ISBN: 978-1-5320-5066-4 (sc)
ISBN: 978-1-5320-5067-1 (e)

Print information available on the last page.

iUniverse rev. date: 05/31/2018

CONTENTS

Chapter 1   Road to Recovery 1

Chapter 2   Breaking News 6

Chapter 3   A Major Discovery 12

Chapter 4   The Halloween Extravaganza 17

Chapter 5   House of Horrors 22

Chapter 6   Death Surface's 28

Chapter 7   The Haunted Maze 34

Chapter 8   Uncharted Territory 40

Chapter 9   Facing Death 46

Chapter 10 Special Effects 52

Chapter 11 The Darkside 58

Chapter 12 The Dungeon Of Doom 64

Chapter 13 Dead Zone 70

Chapter 14 The Many Obstacles 76

Chapter 15 Symbolism 82

Chapter 16 See No Evil 88

Chapter 17 Redefining History 94

Chapter 18 The Past has Return 100

Chapter 19 Mystery of the Maze 106

Chapter 20 Death is Calling 112

Chapter 21   *The Missing Link*..*119*

Chapter 22   *The Final Stage*.. *125*

Chapter 23   *The Mysterious Curse*..*131*

Chapter 24   *The Moment Of Truth*.. *137*

Chapter 25   *The Last Stand*.. *144*

Chapter 26   *The Conclusion* *150*

CHAPTER 1

Road to Recovery

It seems as if the evidences collected that night provided the police with verification. To convict Louis & Eric as the two prime suspects in the halloween murders? Although, there were some speculation on the behalf of Lisa? Who was inform by the killer that the key to all these murders lies hidden between one of the three people she is protecting. Whether it's Jill, Jason or Christian that is held responsible for the murders. Which would sent shock waves across the nation. Considering the influence it may have on others, which spark a fuse within the communities. Of having to deal with fear on that special night in October. Safe to say? That this is a shut close case & that people can finally return to life, as they know it. That after all this time? It seems as if karma play a huge role in revealing Eric's true colors. Along with his partner Louis? Which came as a surprise to Jill, Jason & Christian. Considering his hand in all of this chaos? Which goes to show them that people aren't who they pretend to be? Which is the thing that concerns Lisa about one of them. That has her digging up each one of their background to see what she can find. In results to this case? Meanwhile, the road to recovery seems a bit sketchy. Considering that it's going to take sometime for this sort of thing to blow over. While, the tragedy still remains in the minds of others. Especially, the one's who was affected the most by it all? Which is no one other than Jill, Jason & Christian who had to face the horror. That has haunted them for the past two years.

To make the long story short, sort of speak? The three remain close more than ever. Even though, they are miles away from one another. Considering that this sort of tragedy makes their bondage even stronger. Do to the fact that they have face the nightmare together. Which is sort of like them looking

1

after one another, which is their sworn duty. However, Jill return back to the University she had attended with Amanda & Deshawn. Who will be forever miss dearly in her heart. Jill even decided to stay at the dormroom her & Amanda share together as roommates. Which allows her to reminisce about the good times they had together. Which she often mention to her new roommate Rochelle Mitchell. Rochelle is sort of new to the whole college deal. The fact that she is sort of a outgoing person who is spontaneous in every way. Considering her wits that has Jill enjoying every minute of being in her presence. The two seem delighted by one another's company. They seem so connected with one another that you can almost past them off as being sisters. That's how in sync the two were with each other. Meanwhile, back at their hometown? Christian is closing in on his long term dream of being a newspaper columnist for the local paper company. As his dream will soon be acknowledge throughout the region. When revealing the news to everyone about the truth that went on. Involving the mystery behind the Faces of Death murders. According to his theory of what took place. With the assistance of Lisa who help solve the mystery?

In fact, Lisa stood in touch with all three of them. In order for her to put a lid on things by doing a little investigating of her own. Which would sum up some clues on where each of them stand surrounding this case. That if there is some hidden secret that is confine within the group? It would be Lisa who will be the one to expose the individual held responsible for the murders. That it is her sworn duty to uncover the truth behind the mystery. With that said? Lisa push the issue by keeping taps on each of them hoping that one of them would slip up. Meanwhile, Jason struggle to maintain his composure that contains to life itself? The thing is? That he didn't have no sense of direction where life would take him. The fact that he seems lost at this point in his life. Things would soon change for Jason when a offer was made to him, that he couldn't refuse. An golden opportunity to showcase his skills by doing some advertising for the upcoming Fright`tober Fest. An event that has a certain ring to it, that is showcase around the country each year. Doing the month of October. Which is a amusement park that celebrates halloween like no other. It's one of the most talk about event in the world. The fact that each year it gets bigger & better every time. However, there were some news that this year would include a Haunted House? Which will be added to the park, as it's main attraction. It was Jason's job to get people to take interest in the event by getting the word out. So that the park can sell more tickets which would break the record. For the most people attending an amusement park ever on halloween night.

Which is perfect! Considering the "Grand Opening" of the Haunted House. That has already made headlines across the nation. As one of the most scariest attractions known to man? Which is now trending online as follower's begin to express how elaborating it's going to be? It seems as if Jason two pals got in on the conversation as well. When they seen him on tv doing his thing. Jill & Christian were amaze by their friend's success that they call to congratulate him. To their surprise! Jason manage two free tickets to the haunted house & ask them? Would they accompany him to "The Grand Opening"? They both were lost for words, as they accepted his offer? It seems as if Rochelle got a hold to the good news & wanted to tag along. It would mean the world to Jill to have her bestie be by her side. To share this experience with her. The question was? Is she prepare mentally to handle the pressure of the crowd. Knowing the stipulation which is require for this sort of event. Which is the thing that concerns Rochelle? The fact that either of her two friends are ready to confront their fears. That there is always that moment when the thought enter's their minds. Of what's the chances of this happening again. The thought alone is like a cancer eating away at them. For their sake? Rochelle suggested that maybe they are marked for death. Which was meant as a joke to scare Jill, but in the sense, she knew it to be true. Jill begin to have second thought's about going to the amusement park. As she just had that eerie feeling again. Rochelle then apologize for any inconvenience she may have cause. That she was only joking around with her & that she shouldn't take it to heart.

With a little persuasion Rochelle manage to get through to her by letting her know it's okay. As she joke around some more by taking cheat shots at whoever else wants to be a killer. That they too will feel the wrath of Jill's fury. Refering to her stabbing Eric multiple of times in a violent rage. As Rochelle got her to admit that it felt good to finally nail the bastard. Jill just felt relieve that this thing is over. The fact that she can forget the past & move on with her life. Rochelle couldn't agree more with Jill's statement & quoted the words "Live & Forget"? Which is music to Jill's ears. However, it seems as if all is not forgotten, as Jill was still haunted by the past. As she experience some difficulties later that night. While sleeping? Jill could feel someone's hands being place around her throat. As she starts to gasp for air. Almost as if she is being strangle in her sleep by person's unknown. Which instantly woke her up that led to her gasping *for air. As it turns out that it was only a nightmare she was experiencing. Jill then look over to see if her roommate was in bed. Only to discover that Rochelle was no where's to be found. Which is no big deal? Figuring that maybe she is out somewhere's. Jill then turn to the clock & realize it was only eleven-thirty. She then made her way to the bathroom to gather herself. Although, she still wasn't aware of what's going on? Do to the fact that she isn't full awake. In which the mind is still sleeping that makes it difficult for her to comprehend.*

Which is sort of being unresponsive to certain things the fact that the mind hasn't come too, as of yet. The fact that Jill is unaware of the circumstances, she now face. The instant she click on the bathroom lights & realize that the killer is standing right behind her. You couldn't imagine the fear that consume her, as she gaze into the mirror at the killer. Who is dress in a slicker attire that was worn at this past halloween massacre that took place in the woods. At that point? Jill just totally lost it, as she begin to scream. Which got Rochelle's attention! Which led to her busting through the door to see what is going on. Rochelle try to get Jill to calm down a bit & to show her that it was just a mannequin. Once Jill realize what it was? She begin to take it easy. As Rochelle started to address the issue with the mannequin. Which seem quite amusing considering the explanation behind it. The fact that she confiscated it from one of the janitor's facility. In order to play a cruel joke on someone in her class. Considering that this person deserves it? Do to the fact that the individual come off as being a wise ass. The two begin to chat for a bit then off to sleep they went. In the meanwhile, Christian started to gather the information on the Faces of Death murder case. In order to reveal the mystery to the puzzle. Which would do wonders for his column. Despite the fact that he is being study quite closely by Lisa. Who seems very interested in what he has to say. Containing to the murders he's been apart of? That all of a sudden he wants to write a column about his experience.

Which to Lisa seems like a cop out for resentment of not coming clean. Her only option now is to wait & see where this story leads. Unfortunate, things didn't pan out the way she hope it would. Being that Christian is writing according to how the story was indicated. Based on how it all plays out in the end? Which is sort of a dead end for Lisa. Who would have to wait until this case reach it's verdict on what's the story conclusion. Based on the mystery behind these murders on halloween night. That, until then? She will have to wait on the follow up of Christian's column. Which can take sometime considering how things turn's out? Which is time, Lisa doesn't have? Knowing that she will have to take a different approach. In order to have some success of solving this mystery. However, there were those times where Lisa thought that the killer led her on. By having her going around in circles. Looking for an answer that doesn't comply with the evidences concerning the involvement of Jill & the other two?Figuring that maybe it was all for show to see how far she's willing to go. In order to obtain some kind of explanation that would answer the million dollar question? Which is the game that is being played on her physicality. Now that the two suspects no longer exist. Who came through in a clutch by continuing on with the games, even in death? Being that their plans of wreaking havoc would continue? By punishing those who are mark. Which seems like the only explanation that is reasonable. The fact that the killer wanted her to believe that one of them is the key to unlocking this mystery.

Which kind of play into her weakness of being aggressive when it comes to this sort of thing. In which the killer was testing her to see how far she's willing to go? Even if it means making a sacrifice of betraying the trust of her three friends. By exposing them, in order to gain some kind of purpose. That would result in corruption, as of how the game is decided. According to her perspective of what is true or false. The fact that she could be in denial about this whole situation. Which seems to be the case with Jill, Jason & Christian. It was from that stand point? Of what the killer is attending to accomplish by slandering their names. Which led Lisa to believe that all is well with the three of them. The fact that she was blind by her own ambition to see the truth of the matter. Which was that she let the killer fill her head with all sorts of nonsense. Which affected her better judgement, as of what to believe. From then on, Lisa decided to move on from the case & let the police handle the rest. As they all was in cahoots about what the motives were behind these killings. Jason on the other hand? Seems to be making ends meet. As he started to get a lot of exposure from the camera's by appearing in all sorts of tv interviews. On how well he conducts business in the surrounding area. Making him an overnight sensation in a place he calls home. Somewhere's on the country side of town miles away from the city. Where he can escape the harsh reality of everyday's life in the city. Somewhere's he can lay low for a while, until this whole mess of a nightmare blows over.

CHAPTER 2

Breaking News

Things were starting to look up for the three of them, as time went on. Life itself, seem so amazing of how things are turning out to be? In their quest for a better life of achieving greatness. By turning a bad situation into something more presentable that they all could benefit from? Even though, the nightmares will forever be apart of who they are. As those terrifying memories will be with them forever. Which seems to be the case with Jill. As she had trouble letting go of the past. Do to the fact that somethings will never change. According to Jill who is haunted by it all, considering the fact that someone is taunting her. By leaving her a memoir of past events. Which contains a letter that is written to her as a reminder. That this individual "Knows of a Secret"? Which someone has left on her locker. The note also read on the back, to look inside of her locker. Jill seem skeptical at that point? Not knowing what to expect to happened. As she slowly pull open the locker. About halfway of opening it? Something bizarre happens? When suddenly! Came poping out was a Michael Myers masked. That literally gave Jill an heart attack. As she was stun by the surprise? Especially, by it's sinister laugher that made it more devious. She then, seen that there was another note inside of her locker that said" Gotcha"? It was at that same time when Jill got an unexpected surprise from Rochelle. Who would come off as the person responsible for this little charade. It seems as if Jill couldn't catch a break from all of the nonsense.

Rochelle simply explain that this is the sort of therapy she needs. If she's serious about conquering her fears? That she must embrace the horror that haunts her. To prepare her for what's ahead when she steps inside of the haunted house at the amusement park. Which brings up a great point? Considering the circumstances that all is fair game. When it comes to this sort of thing. That had Rochelle wondering how can Jill manage something of this magnitude. When something simple as a little prank gets her all worked up. That in order for her to enjoy this experience? Jill must step out of her comfort zone & embrace life. The fact that she shouldn't be living in fear all the time. That the time as come to take control of her life. Which is the inspiration Jill needed to hear from someone like Rochelle. A true friend indeed? It was then, when Jill got the message which was very humorous. Which contains to the note saying" I know of a Secret". In which Rochelle seem quite fond of, as one of Jill's many secrets. Which is the tactic she use against Jill to help her face her fears. In order for her to conquer them? From that point on? Jill look at life in a totally different perspective. In which she was tested by the way to see how would she manage under pressure. Which is the thing she needed to overcome her fears. Christian & Jason however, didn't have that problem to worry about. Do to the fact that the nightmare is over. Considering that all is well in hand? Now that the two suspects behind the gruesome murders are no longer a threat to society. As they both seem confident about things concerning the case with Eric & Louis.

Even though, they had their doubts about certain issues that contains to the case. That had them scratching their heads of what was the purpose behind these killings. Considering the possibility that they may never know the reason behind it all. Although, it would be a relief if they had some answers on why this even occur. Of what drove Eric & Louis to commit these horrifying crimes. Which is a mystery in itself? That maybe one day the truth shall be reveal. Meanwhile, on the flip side of things. Jason was selected as one of the few promoters to attend a retail store warehouse convention. That sells all sort of costumes for this upcoming halloween extravaganza. That will be held at the Fright'tober Fest celebration at the amusement park. Jason even went as far as to invite his pal Christian to the event. As a way to support his friend's long term dream of becoming a columnist. Of what a great way to cover a story, then to have this opportunity. To showcase his ability as a upcoming writer. Christian was thrill to have this opportunity to finally showcase what he has learn so far. The two were very eager to see one another. As the timing couldn't be better. Although, it didn't feel the same without Jill being there along with them. Which wasn't a big deal? Considering the fact that they will see her soon enough at the Grand Opening. The convention turn out to be a sensational experience for them both. Until, that moment? When the scary costumes were *being displayed by people who would dare mark them. By having the two of them relive the horror that defines logic.*

Which had them thinking the worse that at precise moment in time. Of all the mindgames being play on them from certain aspect. Which was ingenious! Considering the responds they all got from Jason & Christian. Who seem terrify by it all? Which was the only way for the company to test out their actors. For the haunted house that entitle Jason & Christian participation for this experiment. Do to the fact that they were unaware of what was going on. Until, the owner of the manufacturer broke the news to them. That person being" Mr. Wang Shen" an old weird chinese man that had two entirely different color eyes. Despite the fact that one of his eyes was blue. Considering the fact that it might be dead? While the other one seems to be in perfect shape, which by the way is brown. It was up to Mr. Shen to share his idea's with the world. By using his expertise to help coordinate the features behind the scenes of the haunted house. That would make for great entertainment. Considering that this guy is as good as they get? According to Christian & Jason who were amaze by this guy work ethics. Which would make a great story for Christian's column. As of how much attention this story would get concerning the grand opening of the haunted house. Which would feature some amazing surprises along the way. That there are some high expectations for this year's fright'tober fest. According to Christian's column that has been past on to the public. Thanks too Jason who pull a few strings to get someone to publish his friend article. Which made headlines across the nation.

You couldn't imagine Jill's expression when she saw Christian's column in the paper. That even arouse her curiosity about the upcoming attraction at the Theme park. The word around the nation is that they added something extra to the haunted house. To make things a little more interesting by adding an additional feature to "The House of Horror"? Which is the name that was selected to headline the haunted house. Quoting the words" Enter if you Dare"! Which was all inspired by the great Mr. Shen who is the soul purpose behind this historical event. The word quickly spreaded across the country. As people begin to take interest in what Mr. Shen is offering. A chance of a lifetime to experience halloween like never before. Which seems like fun & games to Jill & her friends. As they couldn't wait to take part in this experience. Considering that they are several months away from being on the grand stage of them all. Meanwhile, the three encounter someone of interest. Who's purpose was to get the inside scoop about their experience. Based on their theory on the murders that relates back to the three of them. This person go's by the name of Raymond Spencer. Who is well aware of the situation containing to the three victims in this case. Raymond knew that he has his work cut out for him. Being a counselor & all? By having each of them bring up the past. Which would begin the healing process to the road of recovery. As he set down with each of them separately to discuss the matter. However, they each demanded that it be off the record.

It seems as if the process is working for the three of them. To obtain some self confidence. In order to embrace the past by accepting it. Which is the first step to recovery by facing the thing that haunts them. Which was the thing Rochelle try to get Jill to see. The fact that talking does help the situation by all means. Which felt like a load has been lifted from deep within. Which means that Raymond has done his job of reviving each one of their spirits. Things begun to get better for the three of them, as time went on. The fact that Jill & her friend Rochelle seems to be connecting with each other on every level. Considering that they are inseparable, which makes the perfect friendship. As they did about everything together. Even though, Jill still kept in touch with her two other friends Jason & Christian. Who by the way? Is taking their careers to new heights. Christian became a journalist for the local newspaper company. The deal was that he would get paid according to how big the story is? Which was just a side deal until, he graduate's college. Knowing that it's just a matter of time before he gets his big break. When he uncovers the truth behind the mysteries of the Faces of Death murders. Then there's Jason? Who is excelling in the marketing department. Who is doing exceptionally well for himself. They all seem to be in good spirits considering how far along they come. It seems as if their dark days are now behind them. Considering how beautiful things are turning out to be? However, there is always that possibility that a storm could be brewing. That maybe it could be the calm before the storm.

Which is the thing that concerns Lisa about certain facts of the story. Almost as if she is being tested, yet again? Feeling as though, something is missing from the case. Even though, she decided to move on from this case & let the authorities handle it. The tempation however? Was too overwhelming not to consider a second look into Eric & Louis files. Lisa couldn't resist the urge of digging even further into uncharted territory. By all means? Taking a look at Eric & Louis background history that may help her get a better understanding about who they were. Lisa then begin the search on the two of them & found some interesting things? That pointed out some key elements to this story. The fact that Eric Johnson had some difficulties coping with the lost of his mother. Considering that his mother was killed in an armed robbery. The suspects however, was never caught by the police. Do to the fact that the suspects made a clean getaway without leaving behind any evidence. As they took full advantage of halloween night. Which is the perfect solution if someone wants to commit a crime. Considering that everyone has on a costume. Which is where things get interesting? Considering this is where Eric got the idea from in the first place. The thought of losing his mother play a huge role in his quest for vengeance. Which is where the Faces of Death masks come in. Which can be perceive as a motive behind these killings. There were other sorts of information that led up to this nightmare. Like, how he was in a conflict with himself about the murder of his mother. That eventually cause him to break down, in which he was place in a psychiatric hospital. For further evaluation?

The doctor who proceeded the treatment on Eric, thought that it was okay to discharge him from the hospital. Which was a bad decision to let him go? Do to the fact that it led to the first onslaughter of murders. That involve some students attending a halloween party. Not to mention the Hatchet family as well. Which is how it all got started, which pretty sums up the rest of the story, as we know it? In Louis case? He became a target, do to the fact that his father was a lawyer. It seems as if his father had made some enemies along the way. By taking bribes from people, as a way to manipulate the system. No matter the terms on whether the person was guilty or not. For the right price he could do wonders. Eventually, he got caught & had to face the conseqences. Which seem like a slap on the wrist from the judge since it was his first offense. Which didn't set well with others. Which was taken out on his family for his wrong doing. The fact that Louis & his mother were made to suffer the consequences. Being that someone in particular found out where the two of them were hiding & decided to take matters into their own hands. Which ended badly for Louis mother who died trying to save her son's life. Not long afterwards? Louis father died mysteriously while in jail. Which gives Louis that motivation to go on a killing spree with Eric. Do to the fact that he was tired of living in fear. And that people disregard his mother's life in the process. The fact that he & his mother had nothing to do with his father's wrong doing. Which was the trigger that gave him a motive to kill. Which was the breaking news, as of how it all traces back to the two of them. Lisa seem so sure that she manage to break open this story. That she feels like she has outdone herself with hard evidences. Which proves that Eric & Louis are indeed the killers. However, if that's really the case, then what role does Jill, Jason & Christian play in all of this?

CHAPTER 3

A Major Discovery

It seems as if Lisa's instincts serves her well pertaining to this case. Now, that majority of the mystery has been solve? The only thing that is missing? Is how it relates to one of the three remaining survivors. In which she is determine to find out at all cost. Meanwhile, Lisa turn to the media with the evidence she collected. Which is her job as an undercover reporter. To report back information based on certain resources she collected. Hoping that the story will flush out the one responsible for these murders. Whether it's Jill, Jason or Christian that is held accountable for these merciless killings. The thing is? That Lisa is going to apply the pressure to the point. Where if they even so much flinch, she was going to tighten up her grip. Even if she have to squeeze the information out of them. In order to get what she wants? That no matter how long it takes, she is going to continue pushing. Until, she gets some answers concerning this case. However, Lisa knew that she would have to do it discreetly. In order to keep the three of them in the dark about what she is doing? In time, all of Lisa's questions would be answer. Containing to the murders that she seems so obsess with. On one stormy night in October, Lisa was on her way home from a meeting she had to attend. Around that time things became grim for Lisa. As her quest for answers in the faces of death murders case, fell on dead ears. The fact that Jill & her two friends didn't show no sign of remorse. Even though, they knew about the story surrounding Eric & Louis. The question was? Is if they are covering for one another.

Which is about to surface? The instant Lisa pull into her driveway. She then, rush to the front door of her house to avoid getting drench. Just as Lisa was headed for the door she stumble on a large envelope. That was on the porch which someone had left for her. On the front of the envelope read "Important documents"? Which right away caught her attention. At that point? Lisa had no idea what the envelope contains too, nor what it consist of? She would soon find out that it contains to the murders. That include a letter & some pictures of Eric, Jason, Raymond & Wang Shen. Along with other pictures of a camaro car & a lady name "Elizabeth Burton"? Which all seems like a bunch of nonsense. Which is where the letter comes in? To get her to see the bigger picture of what is going on? The letter simply explains how the game is to be decided. According to how well she can obtain certain requirements. In order to piece together the mystery behind the chain of events. Which contains to the phrase" Life is a chain, & that every chain has a link"? So the only thing for her to do is to consider each person in the photos, as a potential link in the chain. Which will reveal the truth behind the story. Following the murders of past halloween events. At that point? Lisa knew that her ship has finally come in. That for once & for all? She can put an end to all of this Faces of Death conspiracy. Lisa then, begin to follow up on the issue to see where it would lead too. Which led to a major discovery about what is going on? Based on the role each of them played in the eqaution. Which would determine who the killer is? That is causing all of this mischief.

Lisa has manage a break through in the case, now that she is fully aware of what is going on. Considering that she knows now, what went down, as far as the murders go's? Which brings her to the motive behind the killer's actions? As she made a bee line toward her car to deliver the breaking news to her sponsors. Lisa became an emotional wreck do to the amount of pressure she was under? Do to the circumstances she must have endure psychologically. Of obtaining information surrounding this entire investigation. Lisa seems to be in a hurry to deliver the goods. As she race down the slick wet road, while trying to contact her superior. To inform him about the situation that contains to the Faces of Death murders case. While in the process of calling him? Lisa became distracted by one of the three faces of death masks. That was place on the back sit of the car. At that moment? She knew what was at sake? Considering that the mask symbolize death. Lisa then, starts to panic when someone jumps out in front of her. Causing her to lose control of the vehicle. That sent her into a talespin? Which resulted in a terrible accident. Lisa seem pretty banged up from the crash. As she was steady going in & out of conscious? The fact that one minute she see's the killer dress in the Faces of Death attire. Standing over her, then the next? Spots the paramedics, who is trying to consult with her to see what had *happened? Lisa's last memory was being rush into the emergency room. Before finally, losing consciousness for good. Word had got out to Jill, Jason & Christian about Lisa's car incident. The fact that the police is calling it an unfortunate accident. That there were no physical evidence of foul play in this case.*

They all seem surprise by the news & wanted to see how she was doing. So they all flew down to the hospital where she was stationary at? The three of them come to learn that Lisa has suffer some bad laceration to her body. Along with a couple of broken bones in the process. Do to the fact that the doctors had to perform immediate surgery on her. Although, it wasn't as bad as it seems. Figuring that it could of been much more worse if she didn't have on her seat belt. Which was the thing that save her life? However, the doctor did explain that Lisa is in a very critical, but stable condition. The fact that she will be unresponsive for sometime. Do to the medication he has her on? Which would relieve the pain & have her resting for the time being. The doctor just thought that he should inform the three of them about her condition. Before they go in to see how Lisa is doing? Once they enter the room where Lisa was? They immediately rush to her side. They all begin to sympathize the fact there was nothing they can do. But to tell her how awful they felt that this even happened to her. Not knowing the cause behind this incident? Which would be their undoing when the truth comes out. Of how it would affect each of their lives. Of being unaware that Jason is somehow connected to the halloween murders? Anyhow, Before leaving? Jason decided to give Jill & Christian their free tickets to the "House of Horrors"? Before they departed from one another? That just in a couple of weeks they will be together, once again? Living it up, just like the old times? Which is the perfect setup to blindsided them. Do to the fact that they won't see it coming?

The countdown has already begun to the days remaining in the Grand Opening of "The House of Horrors"? Which is just the therapy they needed to overcome their fears. By accepting halloween as is? That at some point in their life? They would have to face reality. What better way to start? Then by taking some risk? Which is where the haunted house comes into play. Jill & the others seem thrill to experience this once & a lifetime occasion. People from all over the country seem overwhelm by the events that is taking place at this year's Fright'tober Fest. Being that there are some new features that will be presented. Things such as" New Attractions" that will be added to the rides as a extra bonus? Which will add excitement to the whole experience. Not to mention? The House of Horrors that will also be added to the theme park. As one of it's main attractions? Which sort of has a surprising twist added on to it, that would amaze even the people. However, the surprise isn't going to be reveal, until the Grand Opening. Christian even went as far as to do a cover story on the event. In order to share the experience with people the following day after the festivities are over. Which he attends to write in his column after it's been all said & done. Which will be indeed a story for the ages when Jason's dark past catches up to him. Which will reveal his true self on the fact that he has skeletons in the closet? Considering that everything seems peachy for now. Until, that closing moment when the storm comes bearing down on him. In the meanwhile, there were some coverage on the news. Showing footage of the devastation left by the two notorious killers.

Who left their mark on the world with these merciless killings for the past three years. The person of interest behind the crimes was no one other then Eric Johnson. Who police suspected all along? Follow by his partner in crime Louis Tandino? Who committed these murders together. Do to their personal vendetta toward people they condemn. For the pain they had to endure when someone close to them was killed in the same fashion. Which is the truth behind the mystery according to Lisa's story? That now seems inconspicuous based on the new information she received concerning the concept. For how the game is to be decided? The only problem is that she can't past on the information in time. To stop this from happening, all because she is in a hospital recovering. That by the time she recovers, it maybe to late? Which is where the killer's plan comes into full swing. The fact that no one is going to expect a thing. Until, it is too late? However, everyone was under the impression that the killers are no longer a threat to society. The news made that apparent to everyone around the nation. Rochelle found the news to be repulsing to the point where she turn it off. Jill was happy that she did? Do to the fact that she didn't want to hear anymore of the senseless killings, that took place, these past couple of years. Considering that this halloween marks the fourth anniversary. To where it all started three years ago in the first onslaughter of death's. Sending the death toll through the roof.

It seems as if fate is determine to make it hard for the three of them. To commit to something that has tormented them for the longest. That has Jill & Christian kind of skeptical when it comes to halloween. Do to the fact that they are attending college that is filled with a bunch of idiots. Who's soul purpose is too imitate the two killers Eric & Louis. Rochelle seems to be enjoying every minute of it? As Jill was made to suffer the wrath of people's pranks. Rochelle

15

told her? To get use to it, because this is her life now? That she must accept the fact that people are going to behave this way. Which is benefiting Jill? The fact that she can overcome her obstacle. Which is to prepare her for what's to come when she enters the House of Horrors. Jason however, didn't have that problem to worry about. Do to the fact that he now lives in the country. On the other hand? Christian didn't seem all that well with the impostors. Even though, halloween is just a couple of days away. He also knew that the time as come to face his fears. If he is to conquer them? Which is easily said, than done. However, the real test would come when they least expected? Considering that they are unaware of the danger that lurks within. That there is always the possibility the killer could be among those. Who is running around with scary costumes on? That perhaps that certain someone could be watching their every move. Without them knowing what is going on. Which is the perfect cover to go on the prowl. Which is scary in itself.

Considering that the past has come back to haunt them all? Of what the consequences will be? Once the truth gets out that Jason is connected in all of this chaos. Which involves his two friends in the mix, as well? However, there is a time & place, when all is to be reveal. It was just the question of when the opportunity would present itself. That the fate of the game is to be decided by the decision's they make. Which is the test that will decide the outcome to this conclusion? In the meanwhile, Jill & the others were prepare to meet up at the hotel where they would be staying. While, in town for the Fright'tober Fest? In which they will be sharing a room together. They all made it safe to their destination. As they started to greet one another for the first time. Since that time when they all met up at the hospital to see Lisa. Who they kept track of? By having the doctor keep them postdated on her condition. Jill then, introduce Rochelle to her other two friends Jason & Christian. Who seem very eager to meet her acquaintance. After the stories they heard about her. Rochelle also seem please to meet the other two survivors in the Faces of Death murders case. Feeling as though, she is around people she can relate too? As she could almost imagine the hell they all sustain from the misery they had to endure. Which is something the three of them didn't care to discuss at the moment. When there is so much to look forward too. Like venturing out to the theme part. After they get situated with getting check into their hotel room.

CHAPTER 4

The Halloween Extravaganza

After they all got settle putting things away in the room. The celebration had begun with them getting unlimited access to all the rides in the park. Compliments! Of the park's owner, as a favor to Jason for doing a wonderful job. Of advertising this event as the biggest scariest attraction in the nation. Which has brought in more customers than usual. Considering that this could be the year that the record gets broken. For most people attending an event on halloween night at a theme park. Things couldn't get no better than this? As they all seem to be enjoying themselves quite a bit. To the point where Jill, Jason & Christian seem unfazed by all of the scary costumes that is being worn. That's how much fun they were having? The fact that they set aside their concerns & decided to enjoy themselves for a change. Which was expected of them. Which was part of the session that Raymond Spencer recommended. As a way to start the healing process to the road of recovery. Things begin to look up for the days remaining in the upcoming events that follows. Leading up to halloween night where the grand finale takes place. When everyone will witness the "Grand Opening" of The House of Horrors? Everyone seem so eager to know what the big surprise was? That contains to the House of Horrors. Which suppose to be announce at the Grand Opening? Which will come off as huge news to everyone taking part in the event. It seems as if everything is going according to plan. Just as Mr. Shen attended? That soon he is going to unleash hell upon this theme park. Especially, when Raymond's theory is put to the test about the three of them facing their fears.

They all seem quite satisfy with the results so far? Of how amazing this event turn out to be? Even though, the best has yet to come. Do to the fact that they still have three more days to experience life, like ever before. The excitement of it all, is just too overwhelming not to participate in the festivities. Which is the thing that is going to keep people coming back for more. The fact that halloween is drawing near & that the countdown has already begun. That in three days the House of Horrors will be open to the public. Jill & her friends couldn't hardly wait? Until, that moment when they take part in the grandest stage of them all? Even though, there still was some speculations going on with the three of them. As they got some rude awakening along the way. Like for instant? When Christian went to get some ice from the ice machine in the hotel lobby. It seem weird enough that someone was standing at the end of the hallway. Just staring at him? With an insane looking costume on? That gave Christian the willies. However, on his way back to the room? Christian notices that the person in the insane getup. Begin to trace his footsteps? By attempting to make it seems as if he is being stalk by this individual. Who is acting pretty peculiar to Christian. As this person would dare mock him. By trying to insult his intelligence with all of this sneaking around. To the point? Where Christian had enough & decided to confront the individual. Only when he turn around that certain someone had disappear from sight.

However, there was a good chance that Christian knew where the individual ran off too? Considering that the door to the stairways has just shut closed. He then, decided to see where was the individual. By going into the stairway to see if this person is gone. Which appear very strange of how there was no sounds of footsteps going down the stairs. At that point? Christian became fully aware of what is going on. As he made a bee line toward the door. However, when he turn around! There was the individual standing right behind him. Waiting patiently behind the door of the stairway for him to reenter. Clearly, he wasn't expecting that to happened. Which cause him to drop the bucket of ice on the floor. Do to the fact that he was in stock at the time. As it turns out? That it was just a misunderstanding. The fact that it was a teenager playing a game of hide & seek with his brother. Which explains why he was sneaking around like that? Which was a close call for Christian who thought otherwise. Christian return to the room with the news that had them all laughing at him. That the situation itself seem so embarrassing of how humiliating it must have been for him. Not long afterwards they all begin to settle down for the night. As they were exhausted from the kind of day each of them had. They all awoke the next day feeling inspire to do whatever is expected? The fact that they felt free to roam the streets of the city. To get a better view of the town that they are in?

Which will give Christian a better perspective of the city. Something he can add on to his column, besides the amusement park.

They all found the city to be pretty upscale in it's own little way of capturing the tourist's attention. By reflecting some what of the modern times. In which they were intrigued by the history dating back to the early century. That every landmark as a story behind it's historical development. As they come to learn more about what the city has to offer. Besides the fact that it host the Fright'tober Fest each year. As a light bulb then, went off in Christian's head. About writing a column on this particular city history. Which will define logic to this city past reference, throughout it's history. Making it one of the most historical places of their time. As they all spent the hold day researching the city history. They even, went to the museum where they discover a whole lot more information. However, nothing would prepare them for the discovery that was made? While digging for more details that would provide them with a little more insight. Which led them to stumble upon the three Faces of Death masks. That was displayed for everyone to see. Which comes as a total shocker for them all? Of how these three masks relates to this city history. Which seems like one big bombshell has been store upon them. It all seem so astonished to them, as of what they just learn. Prior to it's recent history? That confirms the background of each mask. Stating the fact's that it is indeed" The Urban Killers of Legend"? Which would go on to say? That the three masks is fairly known for it's reputation, as of how they operate.

In critical situations that involves extreme punishment for those who are marked for death. Which was part of a conversation Jill & Rochelle were having. A couple of months ago. About Jill having second thought's on going to the haunted house with her two friends. That literally! Rochelle was right on the money. When she utter the words" Marked for Death"? Which seems kind of weird? Considering the way it was brought up in the conversation. Anyhow, the three of them begin to speculate that this all seems kind of coincidental? Based on the facts that by chance they come to a city where the Faces of Death murders were originated. Which sort of seems a bit Fishy in a way, that got the three of them thinking. That throughout all fifty states this is where they ended up. Which so happens to be by coincidence? Rochelle thought that they were being a little too dramatic about this whole thing. As she suggested that they all take a moment to recollect themselves. As she gave the three of them a reality check. That the persons behind the murders are no longer a threat to them, end of discussion? They all decided to put it behind them, for now? And

continue on with enjoying the rest of their day. As night begins to fall? Jill &
the others took to the halloween extravaganza. By entering the amusement park
for the second time. As they couldn't get enough of all the excitement that is
taking place. Which has them all on the verge of erupting. Do to the amount
of fun they are having. Which sets them apart from their fears of obtaining
some dignity about themselves.

At this point? Jill & the others could care less about the three masks they saw
at the museum. Their only objective is to make good on the promise to accept
life, as is? Which is what they attend to do? By leaving the past behind & to
focus their attention on the next chapter in their life. Which all seem soothing
enough, but the truth of the matter is that? The past will always be consider as
part of the endless cycle that remains to be seen. Sort of like a deer caught in the
headlights. Which is the perfect indication of how it blinds them from seeing the
truth of the matter. That soon enough the past will come back to haunted them
all? Especially, Jason for that matter of how it would affect the outcome to this
mystery. It was just a matter of time before the truth gets out. Which depends on
how quickly Lisa's recovery go's? That would decide how things would turn out.
On whether she can spoil the crime in time, before it even get's started. In the
meanwhile, things was just getting even better for the three of them. As they got
the opportunity to become judges for an event. That has to deal with the costumes
contest. The fact that they are going to be debating which costume is tonight's
big winner. That whoever the winner is? Will receive a check for one thousand
dollars. Not to mention that this will help the three of them get over their fears,
in the process. Even though, the thought still remains in the back of their minds.
The fact that deception plays a huge role on the mind. That has some minor
setbacks of being in total denial. That has the three of them skeptical about this
whole contest. Even though, they decided to go through with it anyway.

In order to prove to themselves that they are ready to conquer their fears by
accepting this challenge. As the costume contest got underway? They then begin
to experience discomfort the further it got into the contest. The whole thing was
just disturbing for them to watch. The fact that there was some gesture that was
made? In which they didn't find very amusing under no circumstances. It almost
seems as if some of them were poking fun at the situation. By taunting the three
of them in the process. Which was just a coincidence by chance? Considering
that it is all for show to convince the crowd to vote for them. Which is kind of
understandable in the minds of Jill, Jason & Christian. Who didn't take it to

heart? Although, they still wasn't aware of the danger that lurks in the shadows. Considering that this person could be one of the contenders in the contest. That is making light of the situation by mocking them. Which is obviously? Part of the killer's strategy to try & control the enviroment. Which is the concept the killer is using, in order to take full advantage of the situation. Which is the element of surprise. Do to the fact that they have no idea what is going on. Eventually, there was a winner who took home the grand prize. While the second & third place winners receive free tickets to the House of Horrors. Later on that night in the hotel? When everyone was relaxing comfortably in their beds. The thought of the three masks had cross Jill's mind. The fact that something doesn't set right with her. As the same thoughts had ran through Christian & Jason's mind, as well. Even though, they kept it to themselves for the time being. Which was something they didn't care to bring up at the moment?

The next day they felt a sudden change within themselves almost as if they were reborn in some way. The fact that they woke up this morning with a different perspective on life itself. Feeling as though, everything is going to be okay. Do to the fact that they are looking forward to today's schedule. Considering that tomorrow is halloween. Which marks the grand finale in the halloween extravaganza. Which will end with a bang? When they all witness the Grand Opening of the House of Horrors tomorrow night. Until then? They decided to go out shopping for souvenirs to take back with them on the way home from the trip. Something to remember this great city legacy? Almost as if they are taking a part of history with them. That would give each of them something to talk or write about considering their experience here. Although, they manage to bypass a couple of imbecile along the way. Who wore scary costumes to intimidate innocent bystanders that cross their path. Mainly tourist for that matter? It would seem as if these young punks get an adrenaline rush off of doing this sort of thing. Which is one way of letting people know that halloween is here. Considering this city foundation of it's history containing too the Faces of Death murders. Which is part of the city historical venue. Dating back to the early century of the modern times. Which is obviously, where the three masks was founded? They all manage to get through the day okay. Without any concerns of doubtfulness. To the three of them it seems like an ordinary day. As they begin to embrace their fears & accept the past for what it is? It was just the process of taking one step at a time.

CHAPTER 5

House of Horrors

They all were eager to see what tomorrow brings, as the celebration continues. The fact that they couldn't hardly wait for the night to pass. So that they can get an early start on venturing through the park. Which fills their excitement with sudden urges of what to expect tomorrow night? When they enter the House of Horrors. Which also comes with a surprising twist in midst of it all? Which is sure to be exciting news of something to rave about in the papers. That has Christian on the edge of what he can gain from all this excitement? Which all seems inspirational to him. To be creative when he expresses the reenactment of the spectacular presentation in his column. In which he has already started by the way. They all were so excited about tomorrow? That it was hard for them to go to sleep. Eventually, they all settle down for the night & drifted off to sleep. The following day was sensational, as the morning sun took to the sky. Which was the alarm that went off in their heads that it is time to wake up. That today marks three years of devastation they had to endure. As they took a moment to pay respect for those who lost their lives in the past years. Which seems to be on everyone's mind at the time. The fact that it was broadcast all over the television. Which was the one thing that brought their spirits down. By having to relive the horror that has haunted them for so long. Of all the friends they have lost in the process. Which is something they will ever forget? No matter how good things are going for them. Which is why they must go through with attending this event? To show their appreciation by not dwelling on the past. Knowing that their friends would want them to move on.

Which is something very sacred to them that Rochelle can definitely relate too. Of all the senseless killings that took place which claim many lives in the process. Which was heartfelt all over the nation. As one of the country's dark times in the past couple of years. Which will be remember, as the Faces of Death murders case. That render the nation with fear of the three masks. Which created so much turmoil within the society of people. Now! That the nightmare is over? People can once again enjoy halloween, as if nothing happened. Which is the thing that will cause their downfall. Do to the fact that they won't see it coming. Which is why? Lisa is in the predicament she is in? Anyhow, the local news station reportedly announce that there will be a tribute for those who lost their lives in these horrific tragedies that occur. In today's special event at the Fright'tober Fest halloween celebration. Which is somethng Jill & her two friends were looking forward too. As a way to show their gratitude for the many victims killed in those incident. Especially, Jason for that matter? Who is somehow connected in all of this chaos? Who is unaware that Lisa knows his secret? It was just a matter of time before the truth gets out. In the meanwhile, they all venture out to the amusement part. To take part in the festivities. As the countdown has already begun to the Grand Opening of the House of Horrors. It seems pretty obvious that the record will be broken by tonight. Do to the large amount of people in attendance this far? There are so much stuff going on at once. That, it was hard for Jill & her friends to decide what intrigue's them the most. As they had a lot of options to choose from? Of all the activities in the surrounding area at their exposure.

They had the choice of riding the scary rollercoasters or playing games in the booth. Which is consider as fun? Do to the fact that they can win prizes in the process. Then, there is always some live entertainment for those who loves music & theatre acts. Which is all part of the celebration, leading up to tonight's big venue. Which is suppose to be a certify sensation like no other. With a bit of a twist to stir things up in light of all the excitement. The expectation was living up to what was expected? Considering all of the hype surrounding this year's Fright'tober Fest. Of being the best one in it's entire history? Which says a lot for the parks reputation of delivering the goods. It was a celebration like no other, as Jill & her friends just took it all in? That it's been a minute since they had fun like this? Which is just the thing they needed to enjoy themselves for once. Taking away all of bad negativity that has clouded their minds for the past two years. The fact that it all seems to good too be true. Considering that they don't have too keep looking over their shoulders. When someone passes them in a scary costume or the fact that? There are a lot of pranking going on around them. Which didn't bother them one bit, as they sort of embrace it. In order to become one with the idea that this is just a phase they are going through. The three of them decided to accept life for what it is? That being? Starting a new chapter in their lives. In hopes, that it will bring them happiness. Which seems to be the case, as of now? However, that still remains to be seen, as a storm is approaching. As trouble is soon to follow nearby? Which will determine how the game is to be decided? Based on the principles of how it all is going to transpires when things begin to unravel.

Of what remains to be seen, once the truth is reveal? That will shatter the mind, of one Jason. Exposing him for who he really is? Which will be discover once Lisa is able to recuperate from her injuries. In the meantime, the moment of truth is drawing near to the Grand Opening of the House of Horrors. Considering that they are a couple of hours away from the big phenomenon. As the crowd begin to pour in the closer it got to the main attraction. Which took the theme park to new heights? As the celebration begun with the news that the record has been broken. Shattering the record by a large margin that tip the scales of production. As the time finally came to reveal the secrets to the House of Horrors latest addition. Which was announce by Mr. Shen who orchestrated this entire venue. As he stands gracefully on the podium to enlighten the people with the surprising announcement. Which is that the haunted house comes with a few surprises along the way. Which was a spoiler alert to some who were dying to know just what are these surprises. Something Mr. Shen didn't reveal to them? Do to the fact that he wanted it to be a surprise. Considering that he can't share any of the details with them. Because it would ruin everything? However, he did mention one minor detail about the haunted house. Which was that it is sort of build like a maze & that they would have to find their way out. The catch to the whole thing is that there are a lot of unexpected surprises along the way. That involves some hidden doors & traps that would be something of interest? Which would capture their attention in ways they never thought possible? Which is consider as a cop out for those who doesn't have the cojones?

To dare enter the asylum, known as, the House of Horrors? However, there is a concept that involves money, as a additional bonus? For those who enter's the House of Horrors. Which would add more fuel to the fire. That whoever makes it out of the haunted house first? Will receive a check for five thousand dollars. Which should persuade them even more to participate in this contest.

It's just the matter of who will make it out first? As Mr. Shen told, them all? To heed the warning that he is going to make it difficult for them to excape. Which thrill the crowd with excitement. As they all seem curious to the thought of being petrify beyond belief? That even had Jill & her friends interested in the concept of taking on this challenge. That by chance? One of them could be the victor in this little competition. Now! That the rules & regulations are in place? The time has come to cut the ribbon to the doors of the House of Horrors. And by the grace of terror! Let the games begin? By having unlimited access to the park. Jason & the others were the first to enter the haunted house. Follow by the crowd who seem eager to step inside of the haunted maze. As a eerie feeling came over them? The instant they step foot inside of the door. Feeling as though, anything can happened at any moment? Which made them cautious about their surrounding that momentarily reminded them of the killers. Who use this method, as a way to hunt down their victims. Which is why the three of them seem so tense. Rochelle try to get them to relax & to just go along with the flow of things. Even though, the haunted house has a way of getting under a person's skin. By the way that it is structure? That would make anyone turn away from it's eerie confinements.

That had Christian wanting out two minutes into the walk through. The fact that it traumatize him on certain levels containing to the similarities of the past two halloween cases. Which freak him out on so many levels of fear. That the thought also enter Jason & Jill's mind that they are not ready for this? As it was a little to late to back out now? Considering that they are now confine within the maze. It all just looks too familiar to them. Almost as if they were experiencing deja'vu all over again by the way this thing is setup. As they begin to get sidetrack from all of the creepy weird sounds. Not knowing what to expected to happened, as a result to all of this craziness? They all took a moment to pause for a second. Just so that they can reset? Once they took the time to gather themselves into believing that they can go through with this? Along with the pep talk they got from Rochelle. Really encourage them to move forward & not let the bitterness of this place get the best of them. As they move along the haunted maze, reality sets in? As of how it all seems unpredictable to what will happened next? Which is the result of fear & how it affects the way the mind function. By having the unexpected to occur when they least expected? Which is scary in itself of how convincing it all seems. Making it by far the scariest attraction ever that was displayed on halloween night. Of how it capture's the spectators attention with it's spine chilling sensation. Which had everyone scary including Jill & her friends. Do to the fact that they don't know what will they encounter next? Considering that it's going to get a lot worse the further they go? Which is where all of the conflict takes place. The fact that reality defines perception when it comes to what is real & what is not?

Which the three of them struggle with, as pose too being realistic about their situation. Containing to the thought of being ridicule in the process, as part of the show. Knowing that this entire venue is based on their experience with fear. Which Mr. Shen use as a guideline to develop the concept for the House of Horrors. Which is why they felt violated? Considering that Mr. Shen use Jason & Christian for personal gain. To obtain the information needed to require absolute greatness. Which would be the perfect replication for the haunted house. Which is just the beginning of their troubles. The fact that they have to deal with the insult. By having to relive though's moments of fear once again. However, the real slap in the face would come when Christian got a video message on his cellphone. That showed a video of him moments eariler in the haunted house. With the song "Every breath you take" playing in the background. The same song he heard that night in the galleria hall. Which alerted him that they are being follow by someone. He then showed the video to the others. They all took offense to the video. As Rochelle wanted to know what sick individual would do such a thing. That only a certain individuals comes to mind when this sort of thing occurs. That being the notorious killers who won't stop at nothing, until they are dead. Which had them all fearful for their lives. As paranoia begins to set in? Even though, none of it made any sense. Do to the fact that Eric & Louis are dead. Meaning that someone is trying to pull one over on him. Jason suggest that he take a look at the number of the person who sent it? Come to find out! That it was Jason all the while long. As a return favor for making an complete ass out of him. One year ago, at the cabin when Christian & Jill pull a similiar prank on him, along with his two buddies Alan & Jerry.

Considering that they might as well go ahead & have fun since there is nothing they can do about the conditions. That this is the sort of thing they needed to conquer their fears. If they are to overcome them. Which is why Jason did what was necessary to get him too lighten up a bit. Even though, Jill & Jason had their concerns as well. It was Jill's who suggested the idea to Jason about getting Christian to see the humor side of it all. Which was psychologically perform on her by Rochelle. That help her see the bigger picture. Which depends on how well she can accept the fact that this is a part of who she is? That once Christian realize the point she is trying to make to him. He too, will begin to understand the process of healing? The fact that he must overcome treachery at all cost. Which is the thing that is constantly hanging over their heads. It was at that moment? Where they decided that enough is enough? Which was the inspiration they needed to continue on with venturing through the haunted house. They experience some very scary things, while searching for a way out of the maze. Of all the booby traps that is conceal throughout the maze. Which made it even scarier do to all of the unexpected surprises they encounter along the way. Which seems very flattering in a way? Considering how it all pertains to the three of them. Based on their experience with fear. Which by the way? Intrigues them! To see what other surprises they have in store for them. Which will be something of interest? That either of them couldn't fathom beyond their wildest dream. Of what lies ahead waiting on them in the confines of the haunted house. That soon they will be face with a decision that will haunt them forever? Considering how things play out in the end that will decided the outcome of the game.

CHAPTER 6

Death Surface's

Which would put a spin on how things manifest once the truth gets out? In the meanwhile, things just seem dandy at this point, up until? Jill receive a phone call from an unknown number that seem pretty out of the ordinary the moment she answer the call. It seems as if she was talking to herself by having to hear echo's of her voice repeating every word she says? Which seems kind of strange? Do to the issue that it didn't make no sense of having to hear herself talk. Considering that the only reponds she was getting was an echo? So Jill decided to end the call, as she thought nothing of it, at the time. It wasn't until, she receive a text message that said" Follow the signs"? That really made her suspicious! Of what this person mean by" Following the signs"? Then it dawned on her that this is just another one of Jason's pranks. Figuring that Jason wanted to get back at her as well. Even though, he deny having anything to do with it? When she confronted him about it. Which only leaves Rochelle & Christian who she didn't leave out. As possible suspect in this case? Knowing that the two of them have more than enough reason to return a favor. Considering that Rochelle likes being spontaneous in these sort of situations. Which leaves Christian who is consider as a slickster by wanting payback. They too? Deny having any part of seeking retribution toward her. Which made Jill furious at the three of them for not coming forward. By not admitting to the true that it was one of them who is playing games with her. That they are doing this out of spite to try & scary her. They all didn't know what she was talking about? So Jill decided to show them the text message left on her phone. That had suddenly been erased from her phone? Making her out to be a liar.

She could of sworn that it was there a minute ago? Which didn't make any sense. As of how the message was deleted from her phone. Which is sort of mindboggling to the point where she suspects that something is wrong. As Jill begin to observe what is going on around her. That trigger something inside of her the instant she begin to look for signs. Which verify some key elements in the equation. That simulate certain aspects of what is to be determine? From all of the pranking that is going on? Which was one way to signal her about the comparison pertaining to the similarity to last year's halloween extravaganza. Which has put her on high alert that the killer is still amongst them. Which puts them in a bad predicament considering where they are? The fact that they are confine within the haunted house structure. Making the situation that much difficult to analyze. As Jill try explaining the situation to the others about what is going on? In which they joke around with her. By telling Jill that it is all in her head? As Rochelle reminded her that the killers are dead. That where is no need to worry about the past. Which is the thing that concerns her the most about this whole setup. As she was convince that the killer is still lurking around. Figuring that Christian had the right frame of mind. By wanting to leave the House of Horrors. Jason had felt the need to console her. By putting his arm around her & to let her know that it is okay. It was comforting to Jill to see that Jason still had the magic touch. That is soothing to her, as of how gentle he can be? When he is not being a jerk? However, the joke would be on her once she discovers the truth of the matter.

Even though, she appears to be okay? The thought alone was too precise to indicate any speculation of foul play. On Jason's behalf on being a part of the prank. However, Jill did have her suspicion about a certain individual. Who appears as an alleged stalker wearing a hideous costume that freak Jill out. This person would come off as a freak of nature. Who seems pretty far out from anything they seen, so far. Making them all feel a bit uncomfortable. As Jason made a suggestion that it is part of the show. Jill thought differently on the matter & suggested that they all find a way out while they still can? Before it is too late? It was at that precise moment? When the lights became a factor. As it begins to flicker constantly, that cause all sorts of chaos within the surrounding area. Making the situation more intense! As they begin to hear voices of their names being call in the distances. Follow by a sinister laughter that symbolize treachery. Of the sound of people being slaughter nearby. Which was terrifying to Jill as she became disoriented by it all? As she struggle to figure out who was who? While searching for her friends in the mayhem. Jill was so petrify by the chaos that she became traumatize by the experience. Leaving her vulnerable to an unexpected attack. As the killer saw the opportunity to take her out of the equation. Which indicated the type of fear that would leave a person speechless? It seems as if she was being torture in a way. By the surprise sneak attack that render her helpless. Just when Jill thought that it couldn't get any worse? The unexpected happens when she got the surprise of a life time? As it turns out? Jill was part of a procedure that would demonstrate the contents of fear. That was all portrayed by Jason who orchestrated the whole thing. Along with his new found friends Marcus & Jerome who took part in the haunted house lineup, as actors.

Even though, Christian & Rochelle was left in the dark about the whole thing. As they too were scare out of their minds by the prank. They all let out a sign of relief once they realize that they are not in danger. Come to find out? That it was Marcus wearing the hideous costume that had Jill freaking out? It seems as if Jason was right on the money. When he hired the two of them to manipulate his friends into believing that the killer is still out there. Considering that the two of them are the masters of terror. Jason had met the two of them through Mr. Shen who hired them to coordinate the structure of the haunted house. In order to bring terror to the House of Horrors. Through the image of Mr. Shen's visionary of creativity. The fact that he leads by example? Which is why Mr. Shen is the master mind behind the House of Horrors. Do to the concept that he is brilliant when it comes to this sort of thing. However, with that being said? Jill admitted that they gave her a good scare. Especially, when they call her up on the phone. That resulted in the mindgames of having to hear echos of herself talk on the receiving end. Not to mention the message they manage to delete from her cellphone stating that" She must follow the signs? Which comes as a surprise to Marcus & Jerome who had no idea what she was talking about. Jill thought that the two of them were pulling her leg by denying the fact? When the truth of the matter is that they seem just as lost as her about the call made to her. Containing too what was said? Even though, they did admit to making a prank call to her cellphone. Which didn't go according to what she describe happen. The fact that Marcus gave Jerome clear instructions on what to say.

Jerome had no knowledge what so ever about receiving any instructions from him. Containing to the prank call too Jill's cellphone. Which cause some confusion on the matter? As Marcus was pretty sure he discuss the issue with

Jerome. In which he deny having anything to do with making a prank call to Jill's phone. Marcus was so sure that it was him dress in a dark full length costume. With a hood covering an wooden figure mask that simulated fear. Which dawned on the three of them that the mask Marcus is refering too is the mask of fear. One of the three Faces of Death masks. Which indicated another sign that something is very wrong with this picture. As Jill would go on speculating that the nightmare is far from over? Which would explain the whole concept of the House of Horrors. Jason & the others try to determine who it was dress in the mask of fear attire. Considering that it wasn't Jerome? Clearly there's been a big misunderstanding about all of this? That there is no doubt an explanation for this little mix up. As Marcus told them all? Not to worry because it is probably part of the show. While the others were trying to come up with a explanation that would clarify what happened? It was then, when Jill would receive another text message from the unknown? Expressing that! There is a killer in their midst? Jill became terrify about what she read & decided to show the others. Which sort of backfire in her face when the message she receive was gone. The fact that it just vanish without a trace? Leading the others too believe that she is hallucinating about things that isn't there. That the pressure is starting to get to her. Considering that the haunted house was a bad idea? Being that she & Christian are not fully prepare too handle something such as this? Jill became outrage when no one took her seriously! The fact that she had too beg them to take heed to the warning.

That this whole setup is not by coincidence? Do to the fact that this entire thing has been a setup? From the moment they arrive in this city. That now? She knows what this person met by" Following the signs"? Which so happens that they ended up in the city there the Faces of Death murders was originated. Not to mention the haunted house that is design as a maze. Making it difficult for them to escape the harsh reality that is based on their experience with fear. Which was use to emulate the House of Horrors image. The fact that they were deceive in the process. Which was all part of the killer's plan to lure the three of them into a place. Where it is suitable for this person to control the environment. That like fools? They fell right into the killer's gameplan. Jason & Rochelle told her? That she is being paranoid that she is experiencing some minor setbacks. Which is understandable considering the predicament they are in? Christian also agree with Jill about how this whole thing came about. Which seems pretty out of the ordinary that by chance they ended up here? Of what's the chance of this happening again, that wade heavily on their minds. Considering all that has went on this far? Which has cause a rift between them splitting up. As Jill, Christian & Rochelle decided to find a way out of the haunted maze. While, Jason & his two new found friends Marcus & Jerome continue to explore the confines of the haunted house. It was then? When Jason got the message that all is not forgotten? When someone sent him a picture of the killer Jason from Friday the thirteen movie. Which is a reminder of his true self that is a spitting image. That defines who he is? In result to the truth of the matter. Which is the soul purpose that somethings just doesn't stay buried in the past? That got him thinking about what Jill had said? Of all the speculations leading up to this event. That sent chills down his spine knowing what's at stake.

The thought alone is too overbearing to handle the stipulations of what is require of him. As he too, receive a text message from this mystery person. Telling him to watch a video of his friends who he abandon. Whom the killer has set his or her sights on? That the object of the game is for him to guess what will happened next? Once Jason realize what was going on? He decided to call Jill to tell them that the killer is in pursuit. It seems as if she couldn't hear him. So he decided to call up Christian instead, but the results were the same. Do to all of the noise in haunted house that drowned out the phones. Jason then made the attempt to go after them, but got distracted by a phone call from the killer. Who manipulated him in every way? By the many threats he & his friends are face with? Considering all of the mindgames they must abide by? That there are so many different ways the killer can blend in. As suppose too them detecting this mystery person. Throughout the haunted maze with all of the unexpected surprises along the way. Of the many scary costumes that is recommended to benefit the killer. Which is scary in itself? Of how terrifying it all sounds coming from the killer. That all boils down to the question? Is that, the killer could be anywhere's? Hiding amongst the crowd just as usual. At that point? Things became intense, as Jason begin to observe all that is going on around him. Which made him very uncomfortable. As the killer started to get inside of his head with the sounds of horror. When ask? What is his favorite scary movie of all time? Before hanging up the phone? As Jason's worse fear is about to be determine. On how well he operates under pressure. When things begin to unfold before his eyes. That will decide the fate of his friends very survival?

In the meanwhile, Jill & the others were unaware that they are being followed by the killer. Who is attempting to plan a surprise sneak attack on one of them. However, the killer wanted to make it known to them that they are being hunted. By senting a video to Jill & Christian about what is going on? Which would make it more terrifying too them knowing what's at stake. As their phones begin to vibrate which is to signal them that someone sent them a message. That being the video of them being stalk by the unknown. Which alerted them both to beware of the danger that has surface. In which they come to realize once they heard Jason's message he left on their voicemail. Containing to the same thing that they are being watch by the killer. Which instantly got their attention that they are surrounded by all sorts of scary costumes. That either of them could be the killer. Which cause some concern on Rochelle part? Do to the fact that she had no idea what was happening. As of how to handle this sort of thing? Considering that she too was being watch? As the pressure was starting to get to her as well. Having the idea of feeling the killer's presence in the area. Makes it hard to sustain any kind of composure that would reduce the amount of fear they have succumb too. Not to mention all of the shocking moments? When the unexpected occurs, basically when something or someone jumps out from the depths. Which alone is scary enough? Which is something else they must account for? Considering that the killer could be anywhere's, dress as anyone. Which is the thing that will haunt them the most about this whole concept. The thought of being preyed upon by a sadistic killer. Who loves too play these sort of games. By tormenting there minds with fear of not knowing when or where the killer will strike. The fact that being inside of a haunted maze doesn't actually help the situation. Do to the fact that they wouldn't see it coming? Which is the perfect image to abide by? Which creates all sorts of turmoil when literally, death comes knocking at the door.

CHAPTER 7

The Haunted Maze

The fact that fear comes in all sorts of forms which is the establishment use to torment them. Which is too overwhelming for Rochelle who begin to feel the effects of being hunted down. While being, detain within the haunted maze structure that makes it even more terrifying. The fact that they all have become the haunted? Of succumbing to their worse fear of all? The fact that being delusional plays a huge role on the state of mind. Which is too much for Rochelle to deal with. As she couldn't take all of the suspense. It was just a matter of time before she loses it & takes off? Leaving behind her best friend Jill & her buddy Christian. The two of them made the effort to go after her, but got distracted along the way. By a few surprises that render them helpless to a couple of pranks gone wrong. Do to the fact that the killer has gotten inside of their heads. With all of the scary talk? Which is where the killer excel at? By confiscating their minds with all of the scary influence. Of having them believe that anything can happened at any moment. Which is the symbol that determines what is reality? Judging from conclusive evidence that all is not what it attends to be? That makes the situation more complicated on deciding what's fact & what is fiction? That perhaps? This whole thing could be stage as an act to promote this event, for future references? To showcase this spectacular event, as a experience like no other. Which is the aim Mr. Shen was going for when he devoted all of his time researching the lives of Jill, Jason & Christian. Based on their story with the killers. Which was the opening he needed to build the franchise known as' The House of Horrors'? The fact that he was able to reassemble every aspect that went on with the three of them. Which seems like the only explanation that they can come up with. Which would explain this entire situation?

Considering that now? All is well in hand of being aware to the cause. That there is no possible way the killers are still around & the chance of another killer seems, "highly unlikely". It seems as if everything is going according to plan. Just as the killer expected it? The fact that they are blinded by perception which has over clouded their judgement. On what is realistic about certain standpoints that states the obvious? Christian made it obvious to Jason about what is going on? As supposed to all of the stuff that is going on with the three of them. By explaining the details to him over the phone. Jason seem furious to the point where he felt disgusted by it all. Feeling as though, he was part of a sham. In which they didn't take very lightly. As they all found their way back to each other, even though. Jill had a difficult time trying to locate her friend Rochelle. Who she was on the phone with, at the time. Who appear to be lost in the maze, as she struggle to find a way out. Jill recommended that she stay put, until they are able to get too her. However, it seems as if this person insisted on harassing the three of them. By playing mindgames with them over the phone. With video clips of them being the targeted. Which also showed this person carrying a knife. Which is to give them an ultimatum about a certain famous slasher. Who identity remains a secret. In order to make the game a little more exciting by guessing the name of the costume this person has on? Which is creepy in itself? Of trying to locate this person in a dark atmosphere with dozens of costume surrounding them. Which cause a conflict between them, as they debated over whether it is real or not. Which is the question that defines all logic based on fact or fiction qualities. Which is a standard procedure of mind over matter deal. As of what remains to be seen in the eye of the beholder.

It seems as if this person wasn't going to make things easier on them. With all of the unexpected surprises they had to endure in the process of locating this mystery person. The fact that there are people jumping out at them from every angle. Which seems torturing enough? Of having to deal with fear when the unexpected occurs. While constantly being manipulated by the killer who is instigating the issue. By using the people dress in scary costumes as a diversion to carry out his or her plans. Which is the perfect technique to make a statement that death comes in many forms. Which creates turmoil for them all of deciding who amongst the crowd is the killer. Whether it is a spectator or someone working behind the scenes. Which makes it that much difficult to determine who is the perpetrator. That is making things difficult for them to enjoy the show. Then suddenly things took a turn for the worse. When Jill receive a video on her cellphone showing her friend Rochelle trap in a unknown area. Looking for a way out of the maze? When suddenly the killer appears out of nowhere's. Dress in a costume from the Urban Legends sequel movie, the Final Cut. It seems as if Rochelle wasn't aware of the killer's presence at the time. As Jill & the others look on with terror in their eyes of witnessing the murder of Jill's beloved friend. As she fell victim to the killer who stab her multiple of times with the knife he or she was carrying around. The killer then pointed the knife toward the device he or she was recording from? To relate the message that the killer is alive & well. As this person begin to motion the knife across his or her neck. To intimidate them of what they can expected to happened. Which ended the video feed to Jill's cellphone. Which has predicated something far much worse than what was attended. As a bit of concern grew on their faces of what they gotten themselves into?

As the three of them struggle to come to terms about what they just witness. The fact that it all could be just an illusion to see how would they react to such a thing. Which was the only assumption Marcus & Jerome could come up with? As of what took place with their friend Rochelle. The three of them suspects that Marcus & Jerome are holding out on them. That there is more to the story then what was mention to them. Concerning the matter of them being connected to this place known as" The House of Horrors"? Marcus & Jerome decided to tell them the truth about what is going on? Despite the fact that things are starting to get a bit out of control. The two of them begin to explain the situation to them. That this whole charade is part of a procedure to test out Mr. Shen's creation. By having the three of them being put to the test to see how he can benefit from their fears. Which would give him a better understanding on how to make the House of Horrors more intimidating to the audience. Which was recommended to Mr. Shen by someone name Raymond Spencer. Who suggested the idea to help them get over their fears, sort of speech. Which is quite soothing to the cause which is part of the healing process. That the thing with Jill's friend Rochelle is just part of the equation? That they can ensure her that no harm as been done to her friend. The three of them felt betrayed in the process of being deceive. Almost as if they were brought in to be a part of an experiment like lab rats. As they couldn't help, but to feel like one big joke too them. The nerve of them to be disloyal to the people that has lost their lives in the process of these killings. Which tells the story about the two of them. The fact that none of this doesn't concerns them in the least. Which made the three of them disgusted by it all? As they demanded that Marcus & Jerome show them the way out of this nightmare of a place. However, Jill didn't want to leave her friend behind. So she decided to give Rochelle a call to tell her that they are leaving.

Jill became concern when she couldn't get in touch with Rochelle. Which made her question the thought of being lie too about the situation involving her friend. However, that would all change when Rochelle return her call. Jill was relieve when Rochelle name appear on the screen. Feeling as though, everything is well in hand, but to her surprise? She was mislead by the phone call? By thinking that it is Rochelle on the receiving end of the call. When actually, it was the killer who confiscated Rochelle's phone. In order to get inside of Jill's head by playing mindgames with her. Jill was so sure that this is part of some plot to scare them. However, the killer left it up to her too decide for herself on whether it's real or not. By making an example of how ruthless this person can be? That by the snap of this person's fingers? All hell is going to break loose. Leaving them all wondering what is the true concept behind the House of Horrors? That got Jill wondering about Mr. Shen & Raymond Spencer? Who are the master minds behind this little creation. Before ending the call? The killer assure her that she will have a different perspective about reality, once things begin to unfold? That just in a few seconds she will feel the effects of the house of horrors. Which is design according to their fears, which will define all odds. That had Jill wondering? Just what is her greatest fear of all? As the killer begin tormenting her by pointing out the obvious? That there are so many scary costumes being worn. That either of them could be the killer in disguise. Making her believe that this mystery person is nearby watching their every move. Jill instantly try to warn the others about what is going on? Even though, she had to do it discreetly, knowing that the killer is somewhere's around lurking in the shadows.

The pressure was beginning to get to her, as she felt uneasy about crossing paths with strangers. Feeling as if there are eyes watching her, as she makes her way through the maze. Jason on the other hand? Felt as if they have taken it too far? By making things difficult for them to adjust within the system. Which is the technique Mr. Spencer is using to help them over come their fears. Which is doing more harm than good considering that they are in for a rude awakening. That now, has Jason concern over the matter. Along with his two buddies Marcus & Jerome who knew the consequence of those associated with *the three of them. Which is where things begin to get creepy. As they venture through the part of the haunted house where the graveyard is located. That the image seem so realistic to the point where it makes a strong impression. Which makes it terrifying! The fact that there is fog covering the floor which makes it hard for them to see what is underneath. Which is where the surprise comes in? When hands suddenly, comes up from the graves all at once. Grabbing a hold to them all, which is something they wasn't expecting. That resulted to them falling on the surface. Where more hands reach out to pinned them down to the ground. While a person dress as' Leatherface" comes out with a chainsaw. To tear through a person's flesh with the chainsaw. While, pinned down to the ground by the show of hands. The fear that was shown by the three of them was remarkable. Of how quickly they responded to what is perception. As the three struggle to get free from the mechanical arms that had them barricaded to the ground. Somehow they manage to get free before the chainsaw slasher got a hold to them.*

However, it seems as if Jerome wasn't lucky enough to get away from the' Texas Chainsaw killer. Who went for the kill, but do to Jerome's quick thinking. He encounter the killer's attack by using one of the mechanical arms. To shield himself from the chainsaw. That somehow he manage to fend off the killer enough to get away. Even though, he manage to get injure in the process. As Jerome felt the set of teeth on the chainsaw tear into his leg. When he try to fend off the killer? Even though, the cut he sustain wasn't life threatening. Considering the fact that it was just a graze he had suffer. That resulted to him limping away. As the killer retreated through one of the hidden doors. At that moment, they all took off running in the maze. To excape the horror that has risen once again? As they ran through the maze all they could hear was the sound of doors being shut around them. As the haunted maze begin to shift. By changing it's features in order to confuse them. Which is one of the things Mr. Shen contribute as part of the aspect. To make it difficult for those you are seeking a way out, in order to claim the money. Which isn't the thing Jill & the others are concern with? Considering that their main priority is to find a way out of this nightmare of a place. No telling what can happened under these conditions. Of being unable to predict what happens next? Which is something they must abide by? Considering the predicament they are in? Which is that? They are now pawns in the killer's game. Which seems to be one of their biggest issues with the concerns of having unexpected things jump out at them. Which is one of the many advantages the killer has over them that being the element of surprise! Which puts them in a very awkward position.

Considering that they wouldn't be able to determine what is actuality. When it all comes boiling down to figuring out the inner working of the haunted house. Mainly by how it is constructed? Which is the measuring stick to how things are determine. Based on their perception of what is reality? When it comes to facing the truth of the matter. That as of yet? Still remains to be determine? As of how it would all play out in the end? Which seems to be the problem they had to endure of shedding some light on this mystery? As they try to make sense of it? As they were under the impression that the two killers involve in the Halloween murders are no longer a threat. Being that the two identity in the killings were Eric & Louis? Which goes to show them that all is not what it appears to be. That there is some kind of angle predicated behind this story. Which is one of the reasons why the killer preferred this location. In order to bring terror back to a community. Where the killing was originated by the three Faces of Death masks. Of what better way to make a statement than the place where it all begin? Which adds to the concept that deception comes into play. The fact that they were misinformed by the speculations of one Lisa. Who comfirmed to the media that the halloween murders have been subdued. As there were reports stating that there is no cause for concern. Which had the three of them wondering was there more to the story behind Lisa's car crash. Which sort of adds up considering how the story was presented? The fact that she too was under the impression that the threat was over? Just like the three of them thought, as well. Figuring that the killer pick the perfect time to strike at the most rare moments when they least expected. With concerns that this individual has been watching them all along. Planning out the details to lure them in, as part of phase one?

CHAPTER 8

Uncharted Territory

Which got them thinking about this whole situation & how it pertains to the three of them. Considering that they are in the crosshairs of being examine by Raymond & Mr. Shen. Who soul purpose is to initiate the procedure. In order to determine the results to the method use by the two of them. To insinuate the fact of the matter. Which is obviously clear that there are some issues that needed to be resolve. Which is where the two of them comes into play. That had Jill & the others concern about the two of them. In regards to the mischief created by the two of them. Which led the three of them to believe that Raymond & Mr. Shen is somehow involve in what is going on? Then suddenly! It dawned on the three of them. That the two of them are indeed connected to this mystery. As the killer made it obvious to Jill by telling her to "Follow the signs". A message she receive earlier from the killer. Not to mention? The other statement that was made about a killer in their midst. Which was to inform them about what is going on? Considering that this is where it all ends for them. Which was the plan from the start? By using their weaknesses against them. By telling them to face their fears, if they are to conquer them. Which was a load of B.S by Raymond Spencer. Who only objective was to manipulate them into facing their fears. Hoping that they will take the bait by entering the House of Horrors. Where Mr. Shen could make the arrangements for the three of them. By setting up the stage for the final act. In the conclusion of the Faces of Death murders? Which will end in the town where it all started from? Which so happens to be by coincidental? That tells the story of a heinous crime dating back to modern times.

However, there was something else more instinctive that tip them off as well? About the two of them being the actual killers in this conspiracy. Something that ties the two of them with connection to this mystery? Giving them the impression that Mr. Shen & Raymond Spencer wanted the three of them to face their fears. When in reality? They were actual saying" What is your greatest fear of all"? A term the killer uses "frequently", to torment them. Which makes all the sense in the world of how they perceive things. When they begin to see the bigger picture of what been place in front of them. That entitle them to kind of get a better understanding about what is going on? Even though, the killers is making an exception to the cause. Before the curtain goes up on this little act. By all means? Making preparation for their untimely death which will make headlines. Once the truth is reveal to the public about why this is happening. In the meanwhile, things begin to take a turn for the worse, as they move along the haunted maze. The fact that it seem much more scarier? Now, that they are aware that their are killers hiding amongst them. That by chance the killer could be right beside them & they won't even know it? Which is why they must remain cautious at all times. Given the fact that anything can happened that any moment. Which is the reality they must face? Which makes things difficult for them? The fact that they know the identity of the people involve. Even though, they have no knowledge of what costume the two of them are wearing. Which is very confusing to them of what to look for? Knowing that the killers love to play games by switching costumes. In order to showcase their dominants which infatuates them. By making them seem invincible to people like Jill & her friends.

Considering that they are in uncharted territory of succumbing to the realization that they are marked for death. As the killer sent each of them pictures of one of the three masks. Which tells the story about the three of them. Based on how they are perceived by the masks. That indicates certain aspects to the cause? Which is the prophecy that will decide the outcome to this mystery? That made Marcus & Jerome to believe that one of them is curse. That according to the tale? Legend has it, that whoever seeks vengeance with the Faces of Death masks. Has put a curse on their accuser by marking them for death. The fact that their fate lies within the three masks. Which will determine how they are to be punish. Whether it's by facing their worse fears. Which will result to them being tormented by that fear? Which is where all the pain & suffering comes into play. In result to their death? Which got the two of them wondering about the situation concern the matter with Raymond Spencer &

Eric Johnson. Whom they overheard Raymond Spencer speaking highly of to Mr. Shen? As of how the two of them were in sync with one another. As he made a statement that Eric's death won't be in vain. According to Marcus & Jerome who can testify to these statements made by Mr. Spencer. Which is beginning to make a lot of sense to them. As the pieces are finally starting to come together. Which has Jill concern over the matter of what it may lead too? In result to them following the signs? That has them all on edge, based on the cause & effect method. Jason seem shock by the breaking news. As a bit of concern grew on his face. Which is something the others notices about him?

Tension begins to build as emotions ran wild of what fate has in store for them. Now that, things are starting to becoming clear to them. Not long before than? Christian receive a call from the killer. Who begins to mock him & the others with treachery remarks over the speaker. Which brought up the subject about knowing who the killers are? As Jill & Christian demanded that the two of them show their face. Do to the fact that they know just as well who is behind the mask? Which brings up a great point, considering who is the killer. Based on the fact that the killer could be hiding amongst them. Standing right under their noses the whole time. The fact that this individual is closer than they think? Which made them suspicious of the people around them who seems very rational at this point. By adapting to the environment, as if everything is legit. Which eventually led to the mindgames. As the killer begin patronizing them by getting them all work up. For something that isn't the case, like giving them the run arounds. Searching for a killer in a costume based on the description the killer gives. Which seems pointless at the moment to continue looking for something they already discover. Which brings up the question of how they can be sure who is the perpetrator. When the perception is so misinform that it is without a doubt unclear to assume what is fact or fiction? That the time has come to test that theory based on their assumption. As the killer added one last detail before ending the call. Leaving them with the thought of what is their favorite scary movie of all time. As all of the lights in the maze went dim? Making it hard for them to see what is going on around them. Which resulted in total chaos as things begin to take form around them. As the creatures of the night started to appear in the most unlikely places.

Causing all sorts of commotions within the surrounding area. Making things difficult for Jill & the others to determine the reality between realization & fabrication? As of which famous slasher the two of them are impersonating.

for her to do? Is to finish what she has started by getting rid off the three of them. Which will end at her hands. That their main focus should be getting out of the maze alive. So that, they can alert the authorities about what is going on? Surely they knew that by chance they would have to get pass Ms. Burton, in order to do that? Jason had the mindset that since he cause all of this? It should be him that puts an end to it? Despite what he may have done? Jill & Christian stuck with him in his time of need? To show him that no matter what happens they were going to remain by his side. Which is what he should of done with Ms. Burton? Which is something they couldn't hold against him. Do to the fact that everyone makes mistakes they regret. Especially when you are a teenager? Which is something Ms. Burton doesn't care to hear? That it is going to take a miracle for the three of them to make it out of this place in one peace. Seems as though, the tables has turn on them of not having any knowledge on who to look for? As that part remains a mystery? Until, further notices from Lisa who is the only one who knows what she looks like? Who is already on her way down there? To clear up this little conspiracy concerning the Faces of Death murders case. Even though, now is not the time to concern themselves with Lisa. When they are still stuck in the haunted maze? Considering how in the world they are going to get themselves out of this mess. With the killer hot on their trail? Which is something they need to be worry about? The fact that there is no telling when she may strike? Which is something they need to be concern with? Considering that they must prepare themselves for what's to come?

CHAPTER 19

Mystery of the Maze

Which is how they must go about thing considering that it is just a phase. That is design as a puzzle to set the tone of the game. Which is to test their ability on the fact & fiction theory? Which is the mystery behind the maze that tells the haunting stories of halloween? That is based around the features of the faces of death masks. That symbolize "Fear, Pain & Torment" as it's name brand for the House of Horrors? Which didn't set well with the three of them. As they discover that there are three stages to the torture chamber. That they must get pass in order to exit the maze. Somehow, they manage to get through one of the stages unharm. However, there are still two more that remains. At that point? Jill seem a bit emotional. Considering that she killed an innocent man. That person being Eric Johnson? Who life she took away one year ago from today? Jason try convincing her that it wasn't her fault about what happened to him. Even though, Jill still felt guilty about it? The fact that she consider herself as being a murderer? As she could not longer hold back her tears. Considering that she will have to deal with it for the rest of her life. By having that on her conscience everytime she thinks about it? Jason would then console her by telling her it's okay. That they are going to get through this together. Meanwhile, Christian seem a bit distracted by something that pull his attention away. From the issue containing to Jill's emotional problems. The fact that he saw something he didn't like? As a responds to him backing away very slowly toward Jill & Jason. Which had the two of them wondering just what the deal is with him?

It had gotten to the point where Christian couldn't hardly talk. As he started to point his finger in the direction where he heard voices calling their names in the dark? Which is when the lights started to cut off one by one headed

106

Whether it's from a random selection of scary costumes or something more effective. That defines the odds when it comes to determining which costume the killers has on? Which is a big concern for them, as of what to expect. When reality kicks in? That they are caught in the thick of things. No telling when something can occur within the matter of minutes. Which is where the three masks comes to play. By feeling it's effect of the combination of fear, pain & torment? The fact that they are tormented by the pain of having to face their worse fear of all? Which is being stalk by the unknown? As the situation begins to take a tragic turn when put in a dangerous position. According to their reaction to the torture they had to sustain. When they came a part of the equation of having to experience fear like no other. Having to face the harsh reality of the haunted maze & how it inflicts with a person's mind. Especially, when under the impression that the killers are nearby watching them. Which makes the situation more intense? Of having the capability to sense the killer presence. Everytime they cross paths with someone dress in a scary costume. Even if they encounter someone that comes in contact with them. That makes them suspicious of the individual by thinking that it is the killer. Which makes their predicament much more scarier do to the fact that it is all one big surprise. Of expecting the unexpected to occur of being unable to anticipate what will happened next? Which is the thing that will decide how would they benefit from all of this?

As of determining who are the killers that has them all wrap up in the palm of their hands. Considering that Raymond Spencer & Mr. Shen is the master minds that is running the show. The fact that Jill & the other couldn't show any signs of relief without coming into contact with someone from the shadows. In that defining moment? When something unexpected happens that would come as a total shock to them. Do to the fact that they wasn't expecting it? Thinking the worse case scenario at that particular moment. Words alone, doesn't describe how ironic the situation have become. With all of the misconception that they must content with in the process. Of being ridicule by their supposed to be mentors. Who finds humor in torturing them with these mindgames. Which is something they couldn't understand about this whole ordeal. As of why the two of them are doing this? As they all try to come up with an explanation that would resolve the issue. Then it suddenly hit them? The fact that it was Jill who they were after? Considering that she was the one that killed Eric Johnson. Which all falls on her as the potential victim? As of why Raymond wanted payback for his falling comrade. Which pretty sums up all of the speculation about which one of them is marked for death? Jason seem a bit concern about what is going on? After all? He too is involve in all of this mayhem? According to the documents Lisa had receive just before her unfortunate accident. Which is the question? As of what role does he play in all of this controversy? Which is yet to be determine? However, their main concern was Jill's safely. As they try to come up with some sort of plan to protect Jill. Even though, they are risking their lives in the process.

While the killer is lurking amongst them, waiting in the shadows of darkness. Then it occur to Christian that what the killer was refering too a minute ago on the phone. Pertaining that there is a killer amongst them? Which turns out to be Jill that the killer speaks of? Considering how she stab Eric multiple of times with the broken glass that was in her hands. Which indeed makes her a killer. That all the while they were convince that the killer was somewhere's in the area. Blending in with the crowd as usual, waiting in the shadows to strike. When the whole time it was Jill being refer too as the killer. Which psychologically clutters their mind with all sorts of deception. As of how well they can comprehend to simple details. As the killer use a method called" Psychology" to manipulate them. By flipping the script according to their perception of what is reality. The fact that this whole thing is one big illusion? Considering how they misinterpreted the concept? Which is that Jill is held accountable for each one of them. That led Christian to believe that this is why her best friend Rochelle was killed. Do to the fact that she was curse along with the rest of them. Which is why Jill receive a memo from the killer stating that she "Follow the signs"? Figuring that it doesn't get no simpler than that? By making it plan & simple to them about what is going on? That had Jill amaze of how well he broke it all down. Which was something he pick up from hanging around Lisa most of the time. Before she got caught up in her work, which pretty much tells the story. However, things was still at it's boiling point of deciding what's their next move. Now that they have a better understanding about what is going on? However, the main issue is trying to locate Raymond & Mr. Shen within the haunted maze. Of deciding which costumes the two of them are wearing follow by the hundredth of people in attendance.

While, trying to decide what's the best thing to do at this point? It seems as if they ran into an dead end of the maze where they must choose between five doors. Where it all seems too similar to the three doors that was at the

Galleria Hall. Years back when they had to choose from though's three doors. Which is something Christian will ever forget. Only this time? There was no Faces of Death masks on the doors. Considering that there were three doors to choose from, as susposed to the five doors. Which doesn't quite add up? Also the fact that it's the only way to go at this point. Considering that it's their only options? Do to the fact that they can't turn back because of the way the maze is design. They all was hesitant about which door to go through? Not knowing what awaits them on the otherside? Which is something they must take in consideration. A sudden discomfort came over them, as a eerie song begin to play in the background. As the suspense was killing them of what may happened? According to this song being played overhead. Which basically tells the story that something is bound to happen? They all debated over who will open the door. Fearing that something dreadful is going to take place? Being the tough guy that he is? Jason decided to take the chance. Even though, Jason seem a bit hesitant when he slowly crept open the door. Only to find a statue posing as the "Angel of Death"? Which got Jason's attention about how natural it looks. The fact that you can almost past it off as being real. That led him to reach inside of the door to examine it? However, just as he was in reaching distances of making contact with the statue. Somethng unexpected happens! When he was stun by Jill who grab his arm. While in the process of touching the texture of the sculpture. Which is where everything went completely black?

CHAPTER 9

Facing Death

Putting them all at a disadvantage of being reduce to darkness. As the doors around them begin opening & closing follow by footsteps in the distance. That had them all concern about the uncertainty of having no intellect on what is developing around them? As chaos ensued? As they were left to face the horror that insinuating more conflict. By using every resource to manipulate them. Even if it means? Using the haunted maze as a certify hunting ground for the killers. To remain anonymous within the confines of the people wearing scary costumes? Which is the thing that is so terrifying about this whole setup? The fact that they couldn't tell the differents between what's real & what's not. That the eyes can appear to be deceiving at times. Do to the fact that the mind can play tricks on a person's way of thinking. About a conception that is so misconstrued by the way it is conceived? Which is the reality they now face? With all of the madness they had to endure. Of being confine to the darkness, while being stalk by the unknown? That had them all on the verge of a meltdown. When something unexpected happens? Making them an emotional wreck each time they come in contact with someone wearing a scary mask. Who attempts to stab them with some sort of knife. That had them thinking the worse case scenario. That any of the performers pretending to be killers. Could actually be consider as the real one by adapting to the surrounding. Which makes all the differents when face with a decision that will determine. Their perception of what is reality? As they must decide which person dress in a scary costume is the killer.

Finally! Things had begun to die down a bit as the lighting in the room return to it's normal setting. Even though, the lights were set at a lower standard. To sustain that eerie sensational feeling of a vibe from the House of Horrors. That insinuate something bad is going to happened. Considering the concept that anything can occur at any moment? Which is something they can expect to happen? That it is inevitable? Considering where they are? They all look around to see if everyone was okay & discover that Jason was missing? Which seems highly unusual considering how it all transpire. Of how he was in the process of observing the output of the statue formerly known as" The Angel of Death? Which is where all of the chaos ensued when suddenly the room went black. Which led Jill & the others to believe that they all were deceive by an illusion. That determines the realization of deception? Based on their concept of how they look at certain things. Which resulted in chaos? As the four of them try to determine what happened to Jason? Considering the fact that they have no idea whether he was dead or not? Which is the question that is on everyone's mind. The fact that he seem affected by it all? Which is the thing that worries them the most about him? The fact that he is all alone wandering around the haunted maze. With the killers who is in hot pursuit of them? That had Jill & Christian concern about their friend Jason? However, they still had to make a decision on what door to go through. Which would indicate their friend's where'a'bouts? Considering that Jason is somewhere's confine within one of the five doors. That in order to find him they must each choose a door. Which seems like their only option at this point? Which had them debating the issue on whether it is in their best interest?

To search for Jason, not knowing his predicament on whether he is alive or not. Which is the perfect plan to lure them right into the killers hands. Considering the fact that appearance can be deceiving at some point in time. Which is angle the killers are aiming for? In hopes, that they will take the bait? Surely they knew what was at stake? The fact that they are playing right into the killers hand. By considering to go along with these silly antics of a game. In order to see where it may lead too? Despite the fact that it is their only alternative at this point? If they are too make their way out of the haunted maze. That the only way to escape the confines of the maze is through one of the five doors. Which is uncertain? Considering the path that lies ahead which will determine their fate? Figuring that their best bet is for them to split up. That each of them should choose a door to go through. Which is the perfect diversion to keep the killers off point. By using Jill as the bait considering that it is her they are after. While Christian, Marcus & Jerome try to find a way out of the *maze. Even though, they couldn't help but to feel like this whole setup is part of the entrapment to lure them in? However, they made a few adjustments before departing from one another. Each of them made sure to stay in touch with one another by downloading the walkie talkie on their cellphones. Jill & Christian also advise that they should find a group of people who aren't wearing a costume & stick with them for the time being. Which is the perfect guide to follow it they are to survive this crisis? Not long before than? The four of them would choose a door to go through. In hopes, that it will lead one of them to the end of the maze.*

It seems as if things are much more terrifying when there is no one else around. That there is no greater feeling of being alone trap inside of a haunted maze. Fill with the expectation that something dreadful is going to happened. It was just the matter of when & how it's going to surface? Which is the motive behind the concept that brings on the fear. Which has it's own unique way of tormenting people who are driven by fear. That the effects of it all is just so severe to withstand the pressure. That has inflicted a tremendous amount of pain & anxiety. When facing their greatest fear of all? That express the true nature of the Faces of Death masks. Considering how it is perceive by the way it is presented as a certify urban legend tale. That tells the story behind this event. Which is remarkable? Considering how the House of Horrors was design based on each of the three masks description of Fear, Pain & Torment? Which is a great combination for wreaking havoc? Considering what's a better way to distinguish fear in a more feasible way, then the haunted house. It was like being in an actual horror movie from Jill's standpoint. As she made her way through the treachery halls of the haunted maze. Where she found herself at the mercy of being ridicule by all sorts of distractions. Which had Jill resenting the fact that she made a bad decision on her part. It seems as if things were beginning to look a lot worse for Jill as she went further into the maze. Considering the fact that there seems to be a surprise at every corner? Making her feel very uncomfortable about her surrounding. Just went she thought that it couldn't get no scarier? The unthinkable happens! Whether it's being chase by some ironic person dress in a scary costume. Who suddenly appears out of nowhere's at the last possible moment. When she least expects it or being petrify by the killer's comments that was sent to her phone.

Which initiated conflict, adding more fuel to the fire as it begins to intensify. Once again? Instigating the issue to try & manipulate her into believing something worthwhile? The fact that she is being deceive by the appearance of all the scary costumes. Leading her to believe that any of them could be the killers in disguise. According to the text messages she receive from the killer. Who is exploiting the situation by using mindgames to scare her. Into believing that everyone she comes across wearing a scary costume, is consider as the killer? That states the obvious when there are stabbing going on all around her. By people dress in scary costumes. Who is imitating the actions in which the killer speaks of? Which is the thing that is so terrifying about this whole situation. The fact that Jill doesn't know who is the killer that is within her surrounding. Considering that she couldn't tell the differents between the stabbing. On whether it was real of not? The fact that it all seem so real based on the concept that looks can be deceiving. According to logic that expresses how things appear when the mind starts to play tricks. That inflicts with the way a person distinguish certain aspects about what is really happening? Do to the fact that she must follow the signs just as the killer instructed? In order to figure out what is going on? Jill would soon get another text message saying" I see you"? At that point? Jill had become suspicious of everyone around her who wore a scary costume. It almost seem as if suddenly all eyes was drawn on her. At least the killer made it look that way by bringing it to her attention. It's amazing! Of how the mind can succumb to the hypnosis of being put into an trance.

By the sum of her worse fear becoming a reality do to a little intimidation from the killer. Who words alone? Has a way of persuading a person's mind with all sorts of delusions? That can affect a person's way of thinking? Which seems to be the issue with Jill? As she try to determine what is reality? As she struggle to determine the reality. On whether there are eyes watching her every move or is it perceive in that way. Jill then, contacted Christian on the walkie talkie that was inserted in their cellphone. To let him know that their plan is working? By having the killers come after her. While the three of them search for a way out of the haunted maze. However, things wasn't going as smoothly as she thought? That he too? Was being harass by the killer as well. Follow by Marcus & Jerome who the killer also begin to torment in the process. Making it difficult for the four of them to escape. Do to the fact that the killers has them all in sight. Which really didn't make no sense? Considering the fact that how can the killers be at more than one place. Being that there are two of them. That it is impossible for the two of them to be in all four spots at the same time. Which got Jill thinking about the message she receive from the killer that said"

I see you"? A message they all receive from the killer? It would seems as if they all got the wrong impression about the message left by the killer. The message simply states that" I see you"? Which means that the killer could be watching either one of them. That the message wasn't just for Jill's sake? It was met for all four of them. The question now! Is which of them are the killers after? Which has yet to be determine on who the killers has set their sights on?

It was made clear that one of them are destined to die an horrific death? It was just the matter of mindgames being played on who is the target? Which is mindboggling? Considering the fact that they all are surrounded by scary costumes. Yet alone? The creatures of the night. Who soul purpose is to terrify the audience with absolute fear. That plays directly in the hands of the killers who feeds off the adrenaline. Which is the formula for disaster? Do to the fact that they won't see it coming. Considering the fact that they have been misguided by the many of scary costumes confine within that area. Which makes it difficult for the four of them to determine who is the killer? Not to mention? All of the hidden surprises that is barricaded around them. That they must account for, as well? Which is design to scare the daylights out of someone. Considerng the fact that they wouldn't be expecting it? Which is the thing that is so terrifying about the maze. Given the impression that anything can happened at any moment. Which is something the killers can abide by? As intensity begins to build by the minute for Jill & the others. Who was tormented by the killers many insults? That has conflicted some serious issues with the four of them. As they were made to believe that everyone wearing a scary costume is consider a suspect? There seems to be terror lurking around every corner throughout the maze. Making the four of them feel very uncomfortable about their surrounding. Especially, when something unexpected happens? That would send them over the edge. Fearing the absolute worse at that particular moment? Almost as if the killers are toying around with them. In order to obtain total dominance of having the pleasure to insert fear. As part of the process, in result to their untimely deaths?

They all agree to check up on one another from time to time just to see if everyone is okay. However, there seems to be some difficulties keeping in touch with one another. Being that there are some interruptions with the signals. That somehow their cellphones would pick up other signals & that the lines would get cross. With other cellphones in the area? Which means that they can zero in. On other people's conversation within their range. Which makes things hard for them to tell the differents between who they are talking too?

The fact that they were in the cross of hearing threats being made. That led to some screaming in the process of someone potentially being murder. All the while, they were trying to communicate with each other. Which created a serious problem for them. As they try to determine who it was screaming bloodly murder over the receiver. Whether it was someone from their group or somebody else in the area. The thought alone was too overbearing to withstand the horror that was displayed over the phone speaker. Considering that there's a good chance the screams could be coming from one of them? Which is the thing that concerns Jill on the matter. Of having to hear someone she knows being slaughter over the phone. The fact that she holds herself accountable for the killings of her friends. Given the fact that she regrets that night one year ago when she killed Eric Johnson. Even though, she had no other choice considering that it was either him or her. However, things begin to pick up. As the signal begin to come in clear again. Jill was relieve once she heard Christian's voice. As she begin calling out for the other two? You couldn't imagine the load that was lifted when she got a responds from Marcus. However, the same couldn't be said, about Jerome who was unresponsive to Jill's call?

CHAPTER 10

Special Effects

They try numerous times hoping that they get a responds from Jerome, but fail to do so? The only thing they heard was static coming from the receiver. They came to the conclusion that the person they heard screaming was none other than Jerome. Considering the fact that the poor boy didn't stand a chance against a ruthless sadistic killer. Who enjoys hunting them down by using all sorts of mindgames to puzzle them. In order to create a distrubance within the environment. Something they are very familiar with? As of why the killers are consider as mindhunters. Based on the their technique of using psychology to rattle a person's mind. With all sorts of illusions being thrown into the mix. In order to keep things in perspective? Almost as if being blinded by the special effects. Judging by what is determine from their stand point? Based on the aspect of things & how it is presented to them. When in reality? The perception seems a bit inconclusive? Of not having any knowledge what so ever, about the situation they are in? Except the fact that Mr. Shen & Mr. Spencer put an hex on Jill. Along with her friends for the killing of Eric Johnson. Which is the only explanation that stands out in their minds. About what are the motives behind the killings of her friends. However, that still is to be determine? Do to the fact that this has been going on for quite sometime now. Before, the killing of Eric Johnson. That had Jill & Christian thinking that there's more to the story. Then seeking justices against them for killing Eric? Considering the fact that it all started with him, in the first place? Which had them both thinking the same thing. Which is that Eric is the key to unlocking this mystery? The fact that it all traces back to him?

The fact that evidence has proven throughout history that tells the story about Eric Johnson. Like how he seems to just vanish into thin air. Without any sign of his where'a'bouts? Up until the night of halloween. Where he miraculously shows up in the end? Wearing some sort of scary costume other than the one use for the killings. In order to cover his tracks by using Louis as the decoy. Which was the strategy they use that night in the Galleria Hall. By pretending that he was the victim with that sob sad story he laid on them. About how he was frame for the killings the year before? In which Eric seem convincing enough to pull the wool over their eyes. When the killer aka "Louis" got into a confrontation with Jason. Which was the opening Eric needed to convince the others that he wasn't the killer. However, that little stunt of his didn't work a second time. As he was stop dead in his tracks by Jill who killed him instead? Preventing him from killing anyone else. Thinking to herself that she has put a stop to the halloween murders. However, that theory was inaccurate? Which made the situation much more worse for the three of them? With Jason gone? All that is left is the two of them. With the exception of Marcus who is now consider as a target. The three of them must decide on what to do? Now, that they know where the killers are? Which is where things begin to get interesting? The fact that someone is trying to reach them through the walkie talkie from Jerome's phone. Figuring that maybe it's the killer who has possession of Jerome's cellphone. Immediately! They assume the worse? As of what the killers are planning next? To their surprise it was Jerome who voice they heard on the walkie talkie.

They all were relief that he was okay & that the scream they heard wasn't from him. Although, he did sounded a bit strange on the phone? Jerome thought that it would be a good idea if they know each others location. Just as a precaution? In order to have some sort of idea on where to start looking. Do to the fact that he & Marcus has a bit of insight on the structure of this maze. Even though, it's their first time actually stepping inside of it? That the two of them can kind of figure their way around. According to what section of the haunted house they are in? Which is a mistake that will cost the three of them dearly? As it turns out? That the person they were speaking too, on the walkie talkie. Was none other than the killer who was inpersonating Jerome. In order to seek out the rest of them within the maze? The only thing that stands in their minds now! Is which of them the killers has targeted? Now, that they know for sure that Jerome is dead. Which is that obvious? Considering that all the killer needed was a little information on their where'a'bouts. What better way than to imitate Jerome's voice, as a recommendation. By deceiving the others with that concept? Which makes all the differents? Considering the fact that the killers now knows? The location of each one of them which is a disadvantage. Do to the fact that the killers aka" Mr. Shen & Mr. Spencer" knows the ins & outs of this place. That they can track the three of them down within the matter of minutes. Which is a cause for concern for the three of them. Not to mention? That either of them could be the target? It was just the question of who will be next? As the killers begin to hunt down it's next victim. Already the killers has claim two of their friends lives in the process. With Jason & Jerome already out of the picture?

It seems as if the killers are down to it's final three victims? Taking that each of them are headed down an unknown path that will decide one of their fate. Leading them to come face to face with their worse fears of all? Which is something they all must embrace, one way or another. That the message would be clear to some, more than others? Pertaining to substantial significants of being realistic about certain aspect within the surrounding area. That would shape up to be an experience like no other for Christian. As a constant reminder that the past has come back to haunt him. Taking a life of it's own with the many different forms. As he dares enter's the House of Horrors "Dimension platform"? A place he is all to familiar with? Dating back to the time where he was surrounded by thousands of mirrors. Where it pretty much started for him that night in the galleria hall. That actually resembles the same structure as the one in the galleria hall that night? That the resemblances between the two are unmistakable? Only this time? There seems to be a variety of famous slashers from the past & more. Located all around him in these special effects mirrors, which is a hologram within the interior. Which makes it seems real, as susposed to how it is display from the projector. Giving Christian that same uneasy feeling. He had that night in the galleria hall when he became a victim to his own relection. By the thousands of mirrors surrounding him. Which seems to be the case as of now? Only this time? Christian had to determine fact from fiction? Between what was shown on the projector & reality? The fact that his eyes was deceiving him with all of the special effects from the mirrors. Which made it hard for him to determine what is real?

When there are all sorts of unexpected surprise along the way. Of having people wearing the exact same scary costume that is being displayed in the mirrors. Jumping out at him from unexpected places at the most rare moments!

Which is a very frightening thing to experience. Considering the fact that the mirrors plays a huge role in the killers plan. By confusing Christian with all sorts of different images of famous slashers from the movies. Knowing that there's a good chance the killer can replicate what's being displayed in the mirrors. By using the holograms that is within the mirrors interior. To help benefit the killers from being detected? Which is the cover the killers needed? In order for their plan to work. Everything seem so conspicuous? As of how things are starting to unfold. That led Christian to believe that somewhere's down the line. Mr. Shen has done this sort of thing before. That got him thinking about the galleria hall & how it was setup. Based on the similarity of how the two was constructed? That only then? Would Christian understand the concept of the game. Which is for him to "Follow the Signs" just as the killers recommended Jill to do? To get a bit of a feel about what is going on? Before they fall at the hands of the killers. The same way Lisa did? Considering that this is where it all ends for them. However, the thing that Christian didn't understand about this whole ordeal is what's the purpose behind it all? Of what's the main reason for the murders? Besides the fact that Jill killed Eric in a violent rage. Considering that this has been going on for quite sometime now? That there's more behind this story than what has been reveal so far. However, Christian didn't concern himself with that, at the moment.

Considering that he had more important things to worry about? Like trying to stay alive? While constantly being mimicked by impersonators who's main purpose is to scare people. Which is right up the killers alley. Which is how they can manipulate them? That is the soul purpose behind this whole ordeal of having it all end, in a place where it all begin? Where the legend of the Faces of Death masks was originated. Considering that all three of them are the poster child for the millennium of urban legend tales. Becoming a serious issue with the reality that history repeats itself? Which is why this town is the pinnacle of evolution. Considering how the legend of the Faces of Death conspiracy evolve, as time starts to past over the years? Of all the stories & myths behind the legendary tales of these three masks. That led some people to believe that it was just nothing more than an urban legend tale? Which seems pretty far off? Considering that this is no fairytale that someone just made up to terrify tourist. That these events really took place throughout history. That now? It is back to seek vengeance against those who are marked for death? Something Christian is very familiar with? As he carefully makes his way through the maze? Although, there were a few surprises along the way that got him all riled up. Of being under the influence that the killers are stalking him. Which made things intense for him to be aware of his surrounding. Not knowing when the killer will strike plays a huge role on a person's psyche. Of having that mentality that appearance can be deceving. Especially, by the way people are acting around him with scary costumes on. That there seems to be some sort of bad vibe he is picking up from this rowdy crowd.

In the sense of endangerment that is transpiring around him. That makes him sort of paranoid about people, in general. Who is imitating the killers persona? Considering the fact that what else can he expect from being in a haunted maze. Full of deception that defines all logic. And to think? That this whole charade of an act is all part of some game being played on them. With the exception that there will be consequences that will determine the outcome of the game. Considering that their lives are at stake? As the killer decided to have a little fun with Christian. While, he trys to find a way out of the room with a thousands mirrors. The killer then suggested that they play a game called" Charades"? Where the killer would give him clues about certain aspects that would determine fact or fiction decisions. Based on the concept that states the obvious on what costume does the killer has on? Whether it's someone in the crowd wearing a scary costume or the images in the mirrors. That says otherwise? About the different types of holograms of famous slashers posted inside of the mirrors interior. The fact that he must decide between technology & reality. Considering the fact that death comes in many forms. That he must guess what scary costume the killer has on. According to the description the killer gives? As he knows all so well? That the mirrors aren't conclusive enough to determine it's perception. Based on the special effects that may have some other implications added on to it? Which is something he learn that night in the galleria hall. That things aren't what they pretend to be? With all of the smoking mirrors indicating that something seems a bit off?

With the concept that there could be a two sided mirror just like the one in the galleria hall. Which indicated the disappearance of Thomas & Jasmine that night? Which is something Christian must avoid at all cost. Considering the amount of pressure he is under of trying to figure out which famous slasher is the killer impersonating? Not to mention? The fact that he must watch out for anything unusual such as' Booby traps'? Christian became an emotional wreck of having to search around for the killer. By having him running around like a chicken with it's head cut off. Almost as if the killer was playing him like a fool by giving him the run arounds? Looking for a killer that is probably somewhere's else. Then it suddenly occur to him? That the reason he couldn't locate the killer was that maybe? The killer could be elsewhere's lurking around? Immediately! He contacted Jill to warn her about what maybe headed her way? Jill was surprise by the news & started to paste around looking for anything unusual. She then begin panicking? To the point where it clouded her judgement. Christian try his best to get her to calm down a bit. Telling her that there's a good chance that the killer may not be coming after her? After all? There's Marcus to consider as well? That they should probably warn him as well about what is going on? Christian then put Jill on hold, while he trys to get a hold to Marcus to give him the heads up. Doing that time, Jill cellphone begins to vibrate. Letting her know that someone is trying to get in touch with her. To her surprise! It was none other than Jason who sent her a text message. Jill was excited to hear from him. Finally! Jill felt relieve knowing that he was alright. The message simply stated that he was okay & that he is looking for her. In order to do that? She must send him a signal from her phone so that he can trace it.

CHAPTER 11

The Darkside

Jill became distracted by the text messages she receive from Jason? That she forgot about Christian who was on the other end. Talking to Marcus about what is going on, as of now? Although, he did call her back to warn her that she needs to be on the lookout for anything unusual. No telling what the killers has up their sleeves? Now that they know who is behind the killings? That this whole concept behind the haunted maze is to torture them with fear. Before facing the consequences of their actions which will result in death. That the object of the game is that they never see the light of day again. Considering that this is where it all ends for them? Which is the darkside of it all? However, Christian was determine to not let that happened. It seem as if Jill took the same approach. By letting him know that all four of them are going to find a way out of this hellish place, together. As she later explain the situation concerning Jason who is very much alive. At that point? Christian was thrilled to hear that Jason was okay. The fact that he couldn't imagine Jill's expression when she heard Jason's voice on the phone. It seem as if he got the wrong impression. As Jill explain to Christian that she really didn't speak with him. That he sent her text messages from his cellphone. Right away? Christian knew that something was wrong with this picture? That got him thinking about certain facts? That seems a bit inconclusive of why Jason would send a text message instead of calling? Which seems a bit out of the ordinary, even for him? At that point? Christian begin to question Jill about what was said, between the two of them. Jill simply explain that it was no big deal? That Jason wanted to know her location. So she sent him a signal from her phone so that he can trace it?

Christian question Jill's decision on why would she do such a thing without checking with him first. Knowing the situation that they are in? The fact that the killer is willing to do anything, in order to get to her. Even it if means, using Jason as a resource to defeat the purpose? The fact that the killer is playing right into her weakness. Which makes her seems vulnerable to the deception that is reality. That things aren't always what they seem to be? The fact that the killer try the same thing earlier with Jerome. Come to find out that it was the killer all along pretending to be Jerome on the walkie talkie. Something that Jill should of pickup on. Feeling as though, if she was blindsided by the enemy. However, that still remains to be determine on whether it was really Jason who sent though's text messages to Jill's cellphone. That the only way to find out is to call him & see whether it's him or not? Jill then? Decided to call Jason's cellphone. While, Christian waits on Jill to put him on three way so that he can hear what's going on? They both had that sick feeling of what they may come across? If things turn out bad then what is expected. At first, things seem a bit unusual, as the phone continues to ring. That had them both thinking that the phone was going to go straight to voicemail. Lucky for them? Someone pick up? However, there seems to be no responds from the individual who answer Jason's phone? At that point? They both begin calling for Jason to see if it was him on the phone. All they could hear was a song playing in the background. A song Christian is very familiar with? That tells the story about his long term friend. Who won't stop at nothing to try & get under his skin.

With that stupid song' Every step you take' by Police. That now? Is not the time to joke around. When there are two killers on the loose. Which proves in itself that it is indeed Jason on the phone playing around like he always do? Come to find out? That the person of interest was none other than the killer. Who has possession of Jason's cellphone. Which could only mean one thing? That would sum up the story about Jason's fate. Which now, leaves the two of them with the additional of Marcus? Who is just a spectator? Who got himself involve in something he can't begin to fathom. As the time begins to countdown with every second of determining their fate. As the killer begin strategizing the outcome to this conclusion? Which makes things more interesting concerning the moral of the story. That can play out either way? Based on their decision making? Which will determine each one of their fates? That they must be careful about the choices they make? Considering that they must face adversity along the way, as a result. To the mindgames that plays a huge role in the killers gameplan. Which is mandatory for the killers. Who is willing to use any &

all resources to their advantage. Even, if it means using their own weakness against them? Which seems to be the case as of now? The fact that Jill was so naive about the text messages she receive from Jason? That it apparently? Over clouded her judgement. Which now, puts her in a very awkward position. The fact that the killer has lock on to her location & is now on the prowl. As the killer continues to torment her over the phone. By stating to her that they should play a game of hide & seek? That the object of the game is for her to try & seek him out amongst the crowd of people wearing scary costumes.

While the killer hide amongst them, which would make the game more terrifying. Considering the fact that she has no knowledge what scary attire the killer has on? At that point? Christian made the choice to come after Jill? By recommending that she send him a signal from her cellphone. The same way she did with Jason's phone? So that he can hopefully spoil the killer's plan? However, it seems as if things didn't turn out the way they hope. Considering the fact that they made things even worse. By sending a signal out to Christian's phone. Which was pick up with the killer who now knows his location? Which was something the killers was hoping they do? So that they can killed two birds with one stone. Which now puts them both in a bit of a bid? Considering that the rules now applied for them both, of being pawns in the killers game. However, that didn't stop Christian from going after Jill. As he was determine to get to her before the killer does? Even though, it's at the risk of his own life. Then it occur to him that maybe they should turn off their phones. Which will put an end to this game of hide & seek. That if their phones are off? Then the feeded will be cut & the killers wouldn't be able to track them down. However, that all sounds fine & dandy to Jill, but it seems as if Christian is missing the big picture. After all, it seems as if the killers aka" Mr. Shen & Mr. Spencer" knows the trademarks of this place. That turning off their phones would be a foolish thing for them to do? That they should have some communication between the three of them. Just in case, something was to happened? Which got them thinking about Marcus who is unaware about what is going on? Which was great? Considering the fact that he is better off the less he knows & that the killers main focus is on the two of them.

Which gives him even more time to escape the haunted maze & tell the authorities about what's going on, before it is to late. The killer then begin to mock the two of them with the nursey rhyme from" Nightmare on Elm Street" movie? Which they could hear in the background? While the killer patronize *them over the phone. Jill had just about enough of the small talk & ended the call. Which now leaves her & Christian to talk among themselves. Without any interruptions from the killer who just enjoys wreaking havoc by causing all sorts of conflict? Dangerous as it may seem? The two of them remain on the phone. Which is the only thing that can keep them calm, as of now? Until, it became an issue? When suddenly! there was a bad connection with the phones. Which eventually led to them losing base with one another. Do to the reception in the maze that can interfere with the phones signal. Which also cuts the feeded to Jill's cellphone? Which makes it unable for Christian to track her down. Putting them both in a very bad predicament. Even though, Christian was still persistent on finding Jill? However, he would have to be very cautious, while doing so? Jill on the other hand? Befriended a couple of strangers she had come across, while trying to find a way out of the maze. Which seems like a good idea at the time. Considering the fact that maybe one of them knows the way out? Also that the killer wouldn't dare step foot to her if she is with a group of people. Even though, some of them wore scary costumes. Which kind of arouse her curiosity about who is underneath the mask? Occasionally! They all seem harmless & that the person she was looking for was no where's around. Unfortunately, she didn't feel the same way about other people within her surrounding.*

Jill became very fond of a young couple she had met within the group of people. That she decided to hang with to keep the killer at bay. Jill seem intrigued by their love for one another, which reminded her of the times she spent with Jason. That the comparison is unmistakable? The couple names were Juliana & Travis? It was there first date together. Of what better way to go on a first date then to a halloween extravaganza. Which is the place where many of the young couples hook up? Anyhow, Jill felt safe within the group as she started to meet the people around her. In order to know who they are? Especially, the ones with the scary costumes on? Which also includes Travis who wore a scary costume. Still in all? There were others who wore scary costumes that wasn't in the group. That she must account for as potential suspects. Not to mention? The actors who job is to scare the audience. Which is something else she must watch out for? Which is mind boggling? Considering the fact that the killer is making things difficult for her. To determine fact from fiction with all of the craziness that is going on around her. That either of them could be the killer in disguise? Which eventually led some of them to scatter when something outrageous happens. However, Jill was persistent on staying with the group despite what go's on? That had them all scattering like roaches when the lights became a factor. Which was the only way the killer could get to her. Unfortunately, that wasn't the case? However, when things begin to die down? Jill found that some of the people in the group were missing? Including Juliana boyfriend Travis? Jill begin to get nervous when she heard people screaming in the distance. The fact that she couldn't tell whether it was the scream of excitement or something treacherous? The only thing she notice was a hand full of people running in the opposite direction.

Unfortunately, for Jill? She didn't stand around long enough to find out what was going on? As she high tail it out of there along with everyone else. Come to find out? That it was all part of the show to scare the others. By having them think that something was wrong? Based on Scientific Fact? That when one comes running they all start to run. Just like a stampede when they are startled by something. As it turns out? The people who were missing suddenly turn up. Even, Juliana's boyfriend Travis who just pop out of nowhere's. It seems as if the two of them found their way back to each other. Even though, Travis has been sort of quiet since his return? Considering that he would always knot his head when they talk to him. Which didn't seem like no big deal? Figuring that maybe he wanted to have that scary mentality vibe. So that he can play the role of the scary villain he is dress as? Which is very frightening by the way? Which kind of had Jill on edge about Travis behavior? However, it was just a phase with her as of being too inconspicuous about the different signs given to her. That issue would be resolve when Travis showed affection toward his girlfriend Juliana. That it was so sweet to see the two of them all lovey dovey once again? However, Jill would have to stay focus on the main priority, which is the killer? Who could be anywhere's at this point. Which is a standard procedure for the killer who made his presence felt. When the killer sent Jill another text message from Jason's cellphone. Explaining in plain details about what she is doing. Which is a sign to her that the killer is near watching her every move. Which is a spoiler alert? That she has been spotted by the killer who is somewhere's hiding amongst the crowd.

The crazy thing about this whole ordeal is how close is the killer to her? Which is the question she must ask herself? That was also written in the text message. Things became intense for Jill as she witness all sorts of debacle within the surrounding area. Which made her delusional about people in general who wore scary costumes. Figuring that one of them is the killer in disguise. The fact that she couldn't tell whether the killer was poking fun at her. By torturing her with the mindgames or being realistic on the subject? Either way? It's a recipe for a disaster waiting to happened? Considering that it was made clear to Jill that the killer wanted her to experience the fear of being hunted. Which is mind boggling to say the least? Of being unable to predict what will happened? Lucky for Jill? She had surrounded herself with fellow tourist. Who she can depend on to ensure her well being if she stay confined within the group. As so she thought? Not imagining in her wildest dreams that the killer is closer than she thinks? That the perception seem so misconstrued to the concept. That it literally blinds her from the truth? Which is that the killer is somewhere's nearby watching her. While, in the process of stalking her every move? As the time unfortunately, draws near. It was at that moment? Where Jill would realize how mobile the killers can be? That at the last possible moment? When things started to change inside of the maze. The truth would be reveal about the differents in Travis personality. As love turn to treachery within that split second. As Jill witness the murder of Juliana being stabbed multiple of times by her estranged boyfriend? Who turn out to be the killer after all? It was at that moment when Jill discover the truth about what happened? That made her realize just how close the killer was to her. Which is the thing that is so traumatizing for her to withstand the concept of it all?

CHAPTER 12

The Dungeon Of Doom

Obviously, it was clear that the killer murder Juliana's boyfriend Travis? The moment he went missing for those couple of minutes. Which explains why they couldn't find him when all of the chaos ensued? Not to mention? The differents in his attitude when he suddenly, turn up again? Which seems pretty out of the ordinary at first, but it seems as if appearance can be deceiving at times? As the killer seem to do what is expected? Which is to adapt? Fooling them both into believing that it was Travis who was underneath the mask. When all along it was the killer pretending to be him. Especially, with all of the lovey dovey stuff that was going on between the two of them. That really, pulled the wool over Jill's eyes. As her focus was elsewhere's which go's to show her that all is not what it seems to be? That she needs to be on the look out for any & everything that comes her way. In the meanwhile, Jill main concern was the killer who decided to come after her. The moment the killer finish with Juliana? It seem as if the changing of the maze was a perfect diversion to commit a murder. Do to all of the distraction that is taking place. Which defines all odds? That there is no place she can hide in this sort of atmosphere. Under these conditions? That there's nothing she can do to stop this from happening? Regardless, who she surround herself with? That the fact of the matter? Is that, there is no one the killer can't impersonate or become. Considering that the killers are everyone of no one to be exact? Meaning that they can use the crowd at their disposal. That everyone wearing a costume is a suspect? Considering that either of them could be the killers disguise as your normal citizen. And, the sad thing about it, is that they won't even know what to look for?

Despite all of the scary costumes that must be accounted for? Considering how the killers are waiting to take this thing over. By leaving their mark in history of being halloween's notorious killers. Which is an impression the killers wanted to leave, as part of this towns history? In the meanwhile, Jill found herself in a bit of a predicament. As she was being chase by the killer who has decevie her with the wrong impression. Of being someone else? Which have claim two more lives in the process, do to her actions. That for every action, there's consequences that are reinforce, as a result. At that point? Jill's world had turn upside down. As she couldn't barely take the suspense of having scary moments in this particular case? As the scenery in the maze begins to change along with everything else. Which is the perfect cover for the killer to camouflage along with the environment. Which is where all of the turmoil started? Of having to sort out the killer from everyone else that had on a scary costume. It was at that point? Where a band of people pretended to be killer's. Which was a problem for Jill who had to suffer the wrath of cruelty. Of being victimize by her own fear, which plays a huge part in the scheme of things. The fact that she couldn't locate the killer within the crowd. Which gives her the impression that by now? The killer may have change into another costume. Which is the thing that concerns her the most about this whole situation. Not to mention, that she needs to be on the lookout for the other killer. Who maybe lurking somewhere's nearby? So, Jill did what was necessary? Which is to high tail it out of there. By forcing her way through the crowd to get away from everyone. Even though, there were a couple of surprises along the way. That terrify her, as she made her way through the maze to escape the harsh crowd.

Meanwhile, Christian seem a bit on edge, as he try to stay on base with reality. He then begin to get that creepy vibe as he heads down to" The Dungeon of Doom"? Which is part of the maze main attractions. Which was constructed in the ancient times that had a bit of a eerie feeling to it? The name alone just seems so bizarre & creepy. That it tells the story about this place. Despite the fact that he has yet to step inside of this haunted era of a place. Christian then starts to debate on whether or not he should go through with this? Then again? It's the only option he can choose from? Christian then begin to venture through the Dungeon of Doom. Considering that he had to mentally prepare himself for what's to come? Not knowing the stipulation that comes with this place. Which is to notify him that he needs to be on the lookout for anything unusual? Strangely enough? There seems to be a darkside that comes with the territory. Of all the odd weird little things that makes this place what it is? Seem so medieval of the times where it all dates back to The Dark Ages. Which includes the Faces of Death masks that was on displayed. Along with some other features that was use doing that time. As Christian move further into the Dungeon. He begin to experience some difficulties, as the lights started to flicker. As the sounds of terror surrounded him? Making him feel very uncomfortable about his surrounding. He then begin to back track his steps. As a certain shadow figure appear behind him. Christian who was unaware of the danger behind him. Slowly begins to backup toward it? He then discovers that the Faces of Death masks are now missing from it's display case? Which gives him the impression that he is not alone? Christian then would receive a text message from the killer saying?

What is his favorite scary movie of all times? It was then? When reality would hit? When he heard the sounds of what seems to be a sinister laugher over the loud speakers. That is located all around the Dungeon. Which is creepy in itself? However, the real scare would come when Christian eventually? Bumps into the shadow figure behind him? The reaction from Christian was remarkable? As of how fear can effect a person's mind with terror when in state of shock? Lucky for him? It was just a structure of an ancient armor body suit. That nearly scare him to death? Meanwhile, Christian suffer another close call? When someone grab him from behind? At that point? Christian just lost it. As he made the attempt to free himself from the killer's grib. Only to find out that it was Marcus you pull him aside? To inform him of the good news about the layout of the maze. That he manage to get his hands on the map. As one of the coordinator of the House of Horrors? He has no recollection of how the maze is design from the inside. Since it's his first time venturing through it? However, with the map makes things seem less complicated? The plan now? Is to try & find Jill who is in great danger. From there, it's goodbye", House of Horrors? However, their first priority is making it out of the Dungeon of Doom alive. Christian try constantly to get in touch with Jill. So that she can send him the signal again from her phone. In order for them to reach her in time. Even though, there's a good chance the killer may also pickup the signal. Which is a risk they would have to take? It seems as though, if he wasn't picking up any signal from the phone. Which is consider bad news for the two of them. As time race against them of prolonging what fate has in store for them. The fact that death comes in many forms. Which is something they must watch out for?

While, searching around the maze for Jill who seem pretty occupy at the *moment? It seems as if the Dungeon has a way of latching on to people. Based on the stupidity of others who find humor in scaring people. Which is Christian & Marcus who didn't find it to be amusing. Which is something they must put up with? Knowing the situation they are in? Which by the way wasn't part of the show. There were so many different confinements within the Dungeon structure. That seem to change from time to time. Which all revolves around a clock that is set to change the dungeon's appearance every five minutes. Making it difficult for Christian & Marcus to find their way out? With all of the trap doors & things shifting around the room. Almost as if they were being deceive by all of the different looks they were getting. From the changing of the maze. Not to mention? The scary part of it all? Which is people poping out from unexpected places wearing scary costumes. When the room starts to change prior to the turn of events? Which is something they will never get use too. Do to the fact that they are under the impression that there's a good chance the killer could be one of those individuals. Who is constantly jumping out at the two of them. Which is something they must consider as a possibility? When it comes to the killer who won't stop at nothing, until they are dead. The fact that the killer can take on many forms. Which is the adversity they must face? Which is the reality they must endure. When the two of them came face to face with a person. Who wore the costume of an executioner? Who is hereby certify to carry out the death sentence of those who are condemned.*

Which is a perfect violation of symbolizing the message that they are marked for death. And, what better way to deliver that message than by dressing as the executioner. Who begins to target the two of them with his razor sharp axe in hand. The two of them saw that they were no match no headsman & started to retreat. As Christian & Marcus found themselves in a bit of an dilemma. When suddenly! All of the lights went out & they were left scrambling in the dark. With the killer not far behind them? Which was critical! At this point? Which kind of freak them out a bit. By putting them in a position where it render's them helpless? The two of them seem lost in the dark. As they couldn't determine what was going on around them. As they begin to hear voices in the distance of children whispering some sort of chat. While, at the mercy of the dungeon that is constantly changing every five minutes along with everything else. They then begin to hear footsteps tagging all around them. Almost as if they were being surrounded? Then that's when things begin to get weird? As the whispers begun to get closer follow by a wicked laughter

that had them feeling discomfort. Which also involves rattling of the chains &
banging on the walls. Despite the fact that there were some? Who took it a step
further by running circles around them. That resulted in a loud scream that
stun the both of them? As frightful as it may seem? The worse as yet to come?
Then eventually, things fell on deaf ears, as all of the commotion in the room
stop? And then, there was silence? As the two of them couldn't hear a peep of
a sound nowhere's.

Which is something that concerns them both about the sudden change. The
fact that now, it is too quiet? Which makes them wonder about what is going
on? Christian then ask Marcus to stay close? So that, they wouldn't get separated
from one another. They then begin verturing through the dark dungeon. In
order to stay clear from the killer who would like nothing more than to take
full advantage of this opportunity. However, it would seem as if the odds are
in their favor. Do to the fact that they are together. That if they stay cool & not
be hesitant about the uncertainties? Then they should be able to manage their
way through this nightmare. At that point? It seems as if Marcus was kind of
tugging away at the back of Christian's shirt. Which had Christian concern
on why is he pulling his shirt. That had Christian thinking that something
was wrong. Figuring that maybe he is scare? So, Christian decided to talk to
Marcus, in order to get him to calm down a bit. Even though, he still was
pulling away at his shirt? At that point? It seems as if Marcus was trying to
push Christian's botton. By constantly whispering his name in a very scary tone.
Which upseted Christian, as he begin to lash out at him. That had Marcus
asking Christian? Who in the world is he talking too? Considering that he
heard Marcus voice someplace else. Other than the place he is suspose to be?
Which is right beside him. Which got them both wondering that if they are
apart from one another. Then who it is that is pulling away at Christian's shirt?
Which is the question he must ask himself? That whoever it was pulling his
shirt had stop? Once Christian realize that it wasn't Marcus who was trailing
behind him? Which kind of spook him out a bit? Considering the fact that
Christian was too scare of what he may find. In result to him turning around
to see who it is behind him?

Christian try his best to remain calm, despite the fact that he could feel the
intensity in the air? Of having to experience fear, like no other? That whoever
is behind him is making their presence known? By making some awful weird
sounds that just makes a person wanna cringe with fear. That later boil down

to a horrific scream. That just terrify Christian? Which was something he wasn't expecting? Neither was Marcus for that matter. As the two of them took off running in the dark. Even though, they manage to stay together through it all? However, it would seem as if things were getting a little too intense for the two of them? As they were left to face even more controversy along the way. The fact that things were getting a little more weirder the deeper they went into the dungeon. Until, they stumble upon the nature of the three Faces of Death masks. That the essence of the masks creates such a debacle? As of how it is reconstructed after all these years. Which brings on a significant feature to it's culture. What would express the true concept behind the history of the three masks. The fact that this whole dungeon of doom was design to represent this towns history doing the dark ages. Which gives them a little taste of how it was back then doing those times. With the addition of the modern times that puts a spin on things. Giving them the pleasure to experience fear from both perspective? Of the effects the three masks had back then, according to today's? As they had to experience the different types of symptoms. Of what it was like back then compare to now? The differents in Pain, Fear & Torment which is the symbols that describe each mask. Which has unleash hell upon them both? With it's fury of combining each one of mask symbols. In order for the two of them to experience all three symptoms at once?

CHAPTER 13

Dead Zone

Which is the repercussion they now have to face, considering that this is what the three masks represents. That defines all logic? Pertaining to how the maze was structure to benefit the phase of all three masks. Considering all three of the different stages that tells the story about the distinguishing character of each mask? That is portray as the highlight theme of this year's extravaganza. It seem as if Christian & Marcus have gotten a few surprises along the way. As they try to make their way through the Dungeon of Doom. With a few close calls to be exact? As the two of them try to distinguish fact from fiction. Based on their perception of what is reality? Considering how they conceive certain things that may seem genuine in their eyes. Which can also be portray as a bunch of smoking mirrors. That may not be seen visually? Do to the uncertainty of the many different forms that is insinuated in the process. Which is something Christian is all too familiar with? As of what he experience in the past that appearance can be deceiving. Depending on, what's at stake? Which could mean the differents on how things turn out? That plays a huge role in determining someone's fate. Which is something Christian has learn in the process. Throughout the years he had to put up with these shenanigans. Somehow, they manage their way through the dungeon. To a place call "Darkness Falls"? Which is the part of the maze where things would get interesting for the two of them? Which is consider as the dead zone? This place alone? Was creepy in itself, of how it tends to create that disturbance in the atmosphere. With the thousands of candles being the only lighting. In this entire section of the maze that stretches nearly a half of mile. Almost as if they were walking through an old creepy asylum that had cobwebs located all over the place.

Which is covered with dust, not to mention the stains on the walls that made it more disheartening. As the two of them begin to wonder just what they may come across in this sort environment. The fact that they won't be expecting nothing less from the killers. Who is using the maze as their hunting ground. By using every aspect of the maze as a certify resource to obtain the momentum. Which is the thrill of the game? It wasn't long before than? When Christian would receive a text message from the killer. Who advise him that they need to be cautious about their surrounding. Cause they would never know when something may occur, unexpectedly? Which all boils down too? Is that, they need to keep their eyes open at all cost? Do to the fact that the killer is nearby watching them. Marcus had just about enough with the mindgames & grab Christian's phone. To relate a message of his own. Who by the way? Made a discovery about the number that the killer had call from? Which was from Mr. Shen's cellphone? A number he recognize all to well. Right away, Marcus came up with a plan? Which is to surprise Mr. Shen when he least expect it? As Marcus begin to explain the gameplan to Christian. That when the time comes? When the killer is in position to go on the attack. Which will be when the opportunity present itself. When something bizarre happens & they windup in the middle of a crisis. Where they are mauled by people wearing scary costumes. Which seems to be where the killer likes to show up. Do to the fact that they are not going to know what costume the killer is wearing. Which is where Marcus plan comes into play? That the moment it happens? He is going to call back the number to Mr. Shen's cellphone.

Which will lead them to Mr. Shen who phone will be ringing. That would provide them with the insight about what costume to look for? Despite, the fact that their will be only one phone that rings doing that time. Which will be Mr. Shen's? Regardless of who he surrounds himself with? Which seems like the perfect plan to catch the killer "aka" Mr. Shen in the act. However, there is alway the possibility that their plan may backfire. Do to the fact that the killer may take a different approach? Which is something they must be on the look out for. Depending on the circumstances? Not knowing what will they encounter as a result of doing this? Which may end up bad for the two of them, if they are not careful? That for every action? There would be some repercussions pertaining to those actions? Which didn't seem like no big deal to the two of them. Considering that this isn't something the killer would expect? As time would soon tell whether they made the right choice. Even though, it seems to look as if things didn't turn out the way they hope. As they experience some very weird things. While, slowly walking through the asylum. That almost feels like they are walking through a madhouse. With all of the commotion going on around them. Which seems like an extreme uproar for the mentally disturbed. As they came in contact with some very sick individuals who just made it unpleasant for the two of them. The fact that they were amaze by what they saw. Which didn't set well with them at all? Considering that every time they turn around things just get hectic. Which had them both, running around in circles, from one place to another. As they both were being chase by what seems to be mentally ill patients. Who wore scary masks, while dress in a straitjacket. With the full use of their arms.

Which makes things difficult for Christian & Marcus? Do to the fact that some of these individuals carry weapons. As a result to terrorizing the audience with fear. As they make an attempt to come after them. With knifes, cleavers, machete, even a chainsaw to be exact. Which got them thinking about the killer who is well known for causing chaos? Considering that this is right up the killer's alley. That now is the time for them to be cautious about people, in general? Considering that anyone of these individuals could be the killer. Which is the thing that worries them both? About this whole situation that involves around chaos. There even seems to be some sort of disruption with the lights. Which was cause by an electric current that was use to summon the electric chair. In which someone was being electrocuted in the process. Which was a disturbing site to see, even though, it's not real? It was getting to the point where things were getting out of control. Which was the concept Mr. Shen was aiming for. When he refer this place as the dead zone? Something, Marcus knew all about, do to the fact that he design it? However, he didn't know that it would be this intense? Which gave him more than enough reason to resent it? However, just as things begin to shift in the killer's direction & the stage was set to intervene with the crowd. Just as Marcus predict will happened? Suddenly, turn out to be a blessing in disguise for them both? As the killer sent out another message to Christian's phone. From the same number as before? Which was from Mr. Shen phone. Asking him "What is his greatest fear of all"? That it would be wise for them to" Follow the signs"? Which will determine the basic principles of reality? That when the time comes to making a decision. Would they be able to tell the differents between fact and fiction?

As the killer ended the message with a question? Which is to beware the danger that is lurking within?

It was at that moment, where their plan would come into play. When Marcus call back the number to Mr. Shen's cellphone. Nerves ran high, as they both waited for a phone to ring somewhere's in the crowd? As the two of them stood by listening for the signal. Which would identify the killer amongst the crowd. Then the unthinkable happened? When the plan came through for them. When suddenly, they heard a phone ringing someplace not far off? It was just the matter of following the sound. In order to give them a little bit of insight on what costume is the killer wearing. Which will blow the cover off this whole conspiracy? However, it was a tough task to try & undermine the fact that this whole thing could be a setup. Do to certain issues that lies in their wake. The crowd being one thing, as suspose to other distraction in the area. Which made it even harder for them to track down the killer. That these distractions also pose a danger to them. Which is something they must keep in mind. Which could run interference for the killer who loves playing mindgames. Which can led to uncertainty death if they are not careful? Things had begun to get intense for the two of them. As they try to locate Mr. Shen before the phone stop ringing. Which would be a bummer, if they lose him? Which was unfortunate for them? Being that they couldn't catch him in time before the phone stop ringing. However, it seem as if Christian was persistent on not letting this opportunity past him by? As he made another attempt to call the number again. Seems as though, the second time's was a charm? When again, they heard the phone ringing somewhere's in the distance. Almost as if the person was running away from them. Only this time? They manage to get a better trace on phone's position. Which sounds as if the phone was somewhere's close. Which seems to be in the heart of the asylum. That is center around the asylum's sanctuary.

That had the dealing of an operating room where the doctors susposedly experiment on the patients. Which was all stage to amuse the audience. However, the problem that lies with Christian & Marcus is that they didn't know what was stage & what was not? Which holds a serious problem with the two of them. As they try to locate Mr. Shen's cellphone. Which will eventually lead to him? Although, things didn't turn out the way they had plan? Even though, they manage to find Mr. Shen's cellphone in the process. Which seems to be lying in the middle of the floor. Which is where it stop ringing of course?

That now leads to the question about the killer's where'a'bouts. Knowing that the killer is somewhere's nearby watching? Which almost seems as if they were lure to this area on purpose. That instead of spoiling the surprise of catching Mr. Shen in the act? It seems as if the killer drag them both into another defining moment. Where they would get a dose of reality? About the perception that seems so obvious at the time? That surrounds the issue containing to reality? The decision of determining fact from fiction was the key element of" Following the signs". That would decide the outcome of what is to be determine. Based on the choices they make? Which has yet to be decided on whether they made the right one? Either way, it's a decision they would have to deal with? According to Christian? It was a clever one to be exact? As the two of them took a moment to look through the phone to see what can they find? That would reveal a little bit more about what is going on? Come to find out that Mr. Shen had them all on speed dial. Which also includes a second number to another one of Mr. Shen's cellphone? That seem pretty bizarre? Of why would he have two entirely different phones at his disposal? That had the two of them wondering? Just what type of game is he trying to pull?

Christian was reluctant to call the number to see if Mr. Shen had a second phone? To their surprise? It was the killer who answer the call. Which seems kind of odd? Considering that it was the killer who sent text messages from this phone? Who they thought was Mr. Shen. Do to the fact that this was his cellphone? Only to find out that he has a second phone as a backup. Which got the two of them wondering if it was really Mr. Shen who sent those messages? As they begin to speculate if there's a third killer. Which kind of sounds like, according to the killer. Who sort of talks in riddles to make things more interesting. The fact that they can never be sure about anything the killer says? Do to the fact that this is all one big game to them. That the signs has always been there from the get go? Which is would they be able to tell the differents between fact & fiction. Which is to beware of the danger that lurks within? Sort of like using reverse psychology? Which was the strategy use to lure them right into the killer's hands. Which is the fact of the matter? However, it seems as if their little strategy was all part of the killer's gameplan. Which is to get the two of them to follow the signs? Not knowing what it may lead too, as a result? That the message was made loud & clear that they don't stand a chance. The fact that they are up against the best? According to the killer's words. As the killer announce over the phone that" It's show time"! With that said? All hell broke loose, when the asylum turn into a nightmare. As chaos ensue? All around them with terror. The fact that they were driven insane by their own fear. Of having to stare danger in the face as it approaches them. The fact that they had to deal with a bunch of lunatic who supposedly has been experimented on? Which is all part of the show.

However, there were somethings that weren't part of show that seem a bit odd? Considering how it all seem so realistic to the point where they couldn't tell the difference. On what's real & what's not? Based on what they are witnessing at this point? Then came the moment of truth? When Christian spotted the killer who wore the same costume as before. When they were in the graveyard part of the maze. Where the killler wore the costume of leatherface from the movie" Texas Chainsaw Massacre". Who seem to be approaching him with the chainsaw full in hand. Christian found himself in a very bad predicament as the leatherface killer crank up the chainsaw. At that point? Christian took off running & so did the killer. Who begin chasing him with the chainsaw. On the other hand? Marcus was left all alone by himself? Afraid of what might happened if he moves? It was almost as if he seem lost about what is happening around him. The fact that he didn't know which way to look of determining what to expect. Now that he is caught in the middle of a crisis. That there is so much going on around him? That it's hard for him to concentrate on what's important? Which could mean the differences on whether he lives or die? With that being a strong possibility, as time approaches? Which is something that will not go unnotice? Considering that he had so any close calls, but none would come as close as this one. When the killer basically crept up on him from behind. That the moment he turn around? The killer took a swipe at him with a razor sharp knife. Lucky for Marcus? He manage to dodge the bullet by stepping out of the away. That somehow, he manage to avoid the killer's blade by the skin of his teeth. Thanks to his quick thinking? That instead of killing him, someone else took the fall? Being that this person was standing right in front of him, at the moment? Marcus would then stare into the face of the killer who wore the costume from the moive" Valentine"? Which is a killer who is known for wearing an all black jump suit. With a mask that simulate the characteristic of a baby.

CHAPTER 14

The Many Obstacles

Who slowly begins to approach Marcus in a weird creepy way. Almost as if the killer is on the prowl? At that point? Marcus started to make his way through the harsh crowd. As he was determine to get as far away from the killer, as possible. Which was crucial for Marcus? Considering the many obstacles he had to endure. That left him in the state of panic of how the crowd can have some impact on a person's mind. With all of the scary stuff that is taking place all around him? The fact that he is hellbound by the asylum's experimentations. Which comes in many forms of disguising one's identity. That plays a huge role on a person's psyche. Considering that you can never tell when or where the killer would strike, next? Do to the fact that it is impossible to determine which person in the crowd is the killer. Especially, when there is a third suspect who identity is unknown at this point? Which is something he & Christian's suspects to be the case? Even though, there is a lot of speculations surrounding this case of mistaken identity. Which was proven all to often? By the perception that is misinterpreted? Based on the nature of how things are conceived from different angles. That tells the story about the basic form of reality? Which indicates the truth behind fact or fiction conclusions? Which means? That there's a good chance Marcus could be headed for more danger. Which seems pretty obvious? Based on how things are transpiring around him that makes a statement? As Marcus try getting the attention of others? That theirs a madman on the loose who is after him? Somehow, he manage to draw enough attention to himself? To the point where people thought that he was being delusional? About a killer he describe was after him, who appear to have disappear from site. Which kind of makes him look foolish in a way.

Considering that this is a haunted house & that he should expect this sort of thing. Which is the object of this whole idea? Which seem typical to the rest of them. Of how baleful things can get? Which is the thing that gives them all goosebumps. It seems as if the killer pick the perfect setting to carry out his plans. Do to the fact that no one will suspect a thing. Considering how easily the killers can adapt to these surrounding. That makes it more difficult to sort out the killers who are amongst the crowd of people. Terror would soon strike? As Marcus found himself in a bit of a predicament. When he would get the surprise of a lifetime. When someone play a cruel joke on him. That ended up pretty bad for Marcus who didn't take the joke very kindly. That led to him running into a wall. Do to the fact that he wasn't paying attention to where he was going, at the time. That resulted in a cut on his forehead, which was a mess. Meanwhile, Christian was on the verge of being rip to shreds. By the alleged killer who seems to be chasing him around with a chainsaw. That so happens to be leatherface from the movie" Texas Chainsaw Massacre"? Christian was so distracted by this? That there were other things he didn't see coming? Which would be the defining moment on how things turn out? Based on the reality that is shaping up, as things progress? That ended when Christian came to an abrupt stop? Considering that he was trap with no place to go? The fact that he took a wrong turn in the maze that resulted in a dead end. That the only way to escape is to go back the way he came. Which is block by the killer who is standing in the way? Christian is now a victim of circumstances? Considering how the killer had him corner like a frigthen little mouse. That the only way to escape is to try & get past the killer. Who is standing in the pathway, tormenting him with the chainsaw.

Christian knew that the only way to get by the killer is to come up with a plan. That wouldn't end up disastrous causing him to get injure in the process. However, that is easily said, than done? Considering that the time is at the essence when under pressure. At that point? Christian became a ticking time bomb. As the pressure begins to build with rage of being ridicule by the killer. Who soul purpose is to intimidate those who are fearful for their lives. Which is something that can have repercussion? Considering that it would be highly dangerous to back a frighten person into a corner. Not knowing the effects it may have on a person's mental state? Considering how unstable this person may get when overcome by fear? Which seems to be the case with Christian. Who just flat out lost it, do to the circumstances? As he attempt to take on the killer even with the chainsaw in hand. The killer would then raise up the chainsaw as soon as Christian came charging that him. Christian would soon tackle the killer. Causing him to drop the chainsaw which seems like the perfect opportunity for Christian. To express how he really feels about being provoke all these years by this individual? Christian then begin assaulting this person with the fury of blows to the face. Bystanders instantly intervene by pulling Christian off the victim. However, Christian insisted that they let him go? That this person was trying to kill him with the chainsaw he had? Christian demanded that they take off the mask. That he can assure them that the person behind the mask is Mr. Shen? The man behind the house of horrors that has created the haunted maze? Who is using his own creation to continue on, with the halloween murders. People in general, seem a bit concern about what was brought to their attention. As they all started to feed into the halloween killing frenzy. Once they discover that the person behind the mask wasn't Mr. Shen? That once again, the killer made the two of them look like total fools in public? That had everyone shaking their heads.

Do to the fact that the two of them are taking things way to seriously? That this whole thing is stage to make it all seem real? Which is what the killers want people to believe? So that no one would believe them. Based on the conclusion that there are killers hiding amongst them. Which is the whole concept behind the haunted maze. The fact that this is what a haunted house suspose to be like? According to the people who paid good money to experience this occasion? That they are going about this thing all wrong? Considering how they are all brainwash by the illusion that is reality? Christian saw that their was no point in trying to convince the crowd otherwise. So he & Marcus decided to move along, but without apologizing to the person he attack. It seems as though, Christian may have mistaken him for someone else? Not wanting to draw more attention to themselves. Christian & Marcus took off running to get as far away from the scene, as possible. Once the people discover that someone had been killed. That got people looking at the two of them funny? Considering how the two of them were behaving, that got people talking. The fact that the two of them seem so overwhelm by all of this? That they begin to get paranoid to the point where they thought someone was after them. Which resulted in someone being killed? Which looks as if it was accidental? Which makes the two of them look like a couple of mentally ill psychotics. Which would explain why Christian attack an innocent man. Who pose as no threat to him, even with a chainsaw that wasn't real. Which made people to believe that the same thing happen with Marcus. Only he manage to kill someone in the process. Which makes total sense to the people who witness the two of them. Behaving irrational about a imaginary killer who is after them. Which was the view from everyone's standpoint of what happened?

It seem as if the killer scheme workout perfectly of making them liable for their actions. Which will determine their fates, based on the decision's they have made? That will determinate the outcome for insinuating the circumstances that follows? Which puts Christian & Marcus in the thick of things? That they are victims of circumstances? However, things could be worse, according to the text message sent by the killer. Who show a picture of a place in the maze called" The Torture Chamber"? Below read" Follow the Signs? Which also displayed the three Faces of Death masks. That was worn by three individuals shown entering this place. The two of them had no idea what were the meanings behind those photos. Of what's the purpose for showing them that? Marcus then, located the chamber on the map to show Christian where it was? They would soon find out that this is where they torture the souls of those who dare enters the chamber. That it is by far the scariest attraction yet, according to Marcus? Who knows just what's on the verge & advise that they stay far away from there, at all cost? Christian took heed to Marcus warning about the" Torture Chamber"? Marcus suggested that they take an alternate route around the torture chamber to avoid this place? Even though, it's the best option to go? That would get them out of the maze faster than taking the long route. Which puts them in more danger the longer they stay inside of the maze. Marcus insisted that they go through with it? Which would be way better than going through the torture chamber? However, they still had to find Jill before leaving the maze. Which is another problem they had to deal with. Christian then reach for his phone to call Jill? When suddenly, his phone begins to ring. The phone showed that the call was coming from Jill's cellphone. At first, Christian seem skeptical about answering the call.

Considering how the killer loves to play mindgames with him. That always result in something bad happening? Even though, Christian knew that he must take this call? Do to the fact that he may not get another chance to use the phone? Considering the bad reception he is getting from this place. Christian was afraid of what he might hear, as susposed to what he may encounter over the phone. To his delight, Christian was please to hear Jill's voice again? It *seems as though, she was okay? Jill was also glad to hear that the two of them are okay, as well? That the two of them manage to find their way back to each other. After being split up all this time? Christian then inform her of the good news that Marcus came across a map of the maze. That they are coming get her, so that they can exit this place together. Christian then ask, Jill where is she located inside of the maze? Jill specifically told them, that she was in a place called" The Torture Chamber"? Immediately, Christian knew the reason why the killer sent him those photos? Which would explain a lot about what is going on? Christian ask Jill, how far is she in the chamber? She then replied, that she just enter through the doors three minutes ago. Marcus would then take the phone from Christian's hand. To ask, Jill? Was there anyway she could find her way back out of the chamber? Jill didn't like the sound of Marcus voice. When he ask, her that question? Which made her kind of jittery, when she told him, no? Despite the fact that she could tell that something was wrong. By the sound of Marcus voice? It seems as if Christian & Marcus was at a crossroad of figuring out what to do? Which seems very obvious to Christian that they must go in after her? Despite the fact of how dangerous the torture chamber may seem. That there was no way he was going to leave this place without Jill? Considering that they have been through too much for him to just turn away.*

Jill became concern at that point & wanted to know what is going on? Christian told her to brace herself for what she is about to hear. Because there's no easy way to say this? That would make the situation less stressful. He then begin to explain to her about the danger that lies waiting in the confines of the torture chamber. That she should beware of three individuals wearing the Faces of Death masks. That there's a possibility all three of them could be the killers. Then again, there is always the possibility that this maybe a front. In order to get her focus on something that isn't the case. By distracting her with bogus appearance. Considering how the killers loves to play games by switching things up. That just when they think they have some commom ground on what to look for? It seems as if they are in for a rude awakening when something unexpected happens. Which is the writing on the wall that will insinuate more conflict? That will stand the test of time on analyzing the truth of the matter. Based on their perception of reality? Which may come as a total coincidence? Of how things seems to evolve substantially throughout the night. That will determine how things would play out in the end? That already has some repercussions containing to Christian & Marcus being mentally unstable. To the point where some people witness an attack on an innocent individual who was doing his job. That led them all to believe that it was Marcus who killed a man. As a result to their paranoia. Which was the reality they had to face of being protrayed as the killer. In which, they warn Jill about the different obstacles she now face? That can have many affects according to her actions? They then told her? To stay put, until they are able to reach her. However, she needs to be focus on the things going on around her. Which was the only advice he could give to her at the time.

It seem as if they were racing against time of getting to her before the killer does? It was just the question of who would get to her first? Christian try to stay in touch with her over the phone, but the connection was bad. As they begin to lose base with one another. It was getting so that they couldn't hardly hear each other. It was at that point, where Jill's cellphone had cut off. Do to the fact that she had a low battery. Which made Christian more determined to find her. That their main focus was getting to her in time. Which took their mind off what's important? That they had to be reminded of the terror that can strke instantly! without warning? That led to a few unexpected surprises which got their blood boiling. Which wasn't going to discourage them in the least? Do to the fact that they had their hearts set on finding Jill, no matter the cost? Which brings up the situation involving Jill's case. Who is trap inside the tremendous torture chamber. A place where people are torture by the reality of having to encounter. Some very sadidtic things that would turn a person's stomach upside down. By the way it is structure. That would intimidate any person who come across this site. Which was something Jill didn't pay no attention to because she was on the phone with Christian at the time. However, she could see why Marcus was so terrify of this place. Considering how it just creeps a person out with it's appeal that sends chills down your back. That this is by far the scariest place in the maze. However, the one thing that has affected her the most about this place is the scary sounds. Not to mention, the sudden chill she felt. When she heard something draging across the floor nearby. Whatever it was, scary a whole lot of people who came charging toward her. Screaming at the top of their lungs which seems pretty terrifying? It seems as if Jill didn't stand around to find out what is going on. As she starts to scatter along with everyone else. Knowing that she suppose to stay put, until Christian & Marcus get there?

CHAPTER 15

Symbolism

Jill stop for a moment to reconsider her decision about leaving the area. Knowing that Christian & Marcus are on their way to get her. Which puts her in a very awkward position? That if she leaves the area, then it would make the search much more difficult for Christian & Marcus? Who advice her to stay put, but if she stay's? There's a good chance of her being capture by the killers? Which isn't an option? Considering how the killers can use her as bait to lure in the others. Which is bad no matter how the cut goes? That she is caught in the crosshairs of making a decision based on the deciding factor? That will determine the outcome of her fate. As time was running out for her to come up with a solution. On what's the best thing for her to do right now? Considering how the noise of something being drag across the floor is drawing near. Which sounds like a heavy piece of metal being drag across the floor. Jill started to get goosebumps as she begin to pace around the room. To see where can see hide. In order to stay hidden from god knows what? That is headed her way with something unusual? Which is something she didn't care to find out on what it was? Intensity begins to build, as the noise started to get louder the closer it got to her. Jill quickly hid under a sheet that is covering a large table. Which reach the length of the floor. Which is perfect from being detected by prying eyes? Jill could hear the sounds of metal being drag right in front of her. She could see the shadows of someone's foot walking pass her. Along with the piece of metal this person seems to be draging around. Then without warning! This person started to walk toward where she was hiding & then pause for a moment?

It seems as if this person was standing right over her tapping on the table she was under? The adrenaline then started to kick in, as she cringe with fear.

Afraid that this person knows where she is hiding. That any minute now? This person is going to raise up the sheet & snatch her from under the table. Which is the thought that ran through her mind constantly while this individual stood over her. That had her trembling uncontrollably? To her surprise! The person had started to move along draging behind the massive piece of metal. Jill was relieve when she heard the noise going in the other direction, away from her. As she softly let out a sigh? However, it seem as if something was wrong? When suddenly? This person stop for a brief moment. At that point? Jill seem a bit on edge about why this person stop? That for two whole minutes there was silence. Which got Jill wondering about what is going on? Considering how it all seems miraculous? On how everything just stop within that split second? Jill would then take a peek around the room by lifting up the sheet a little bit. All because she is too afraid to step away from underneath the table. Do to what may happen if she does? Which is the tricky thing about this whole ordeal of not being able to predict what will happen next? Which is the thing that seem so troubling about this whole setup. That got her all jittery for some reason. In the meantime, she found herself occupy with all sorts of question? That has overcloud her mind with speculations? It seems clear enough that there was no one else in the room, besides her. Which seems kind of strange considering how the person that was in the room with her. Manage to pull a disappearing act at the last possible moment. When it was clear that the individual has never left in the first place?

That led her to believe that this person is still around hiding someplace? Jill would then come from under the table to take a look around. However, she was still skeptical about her surrounding? Afraid of what she may encounter in the long run. Considering how peculiar it all seems of the sudden silence that overwhelm her. Which kind of freak her out a little bit considering the many concerns that weigh heavily on her mind. Of the possibility that something bad can happened within a split second? However, nothing could compare to what happens next? That send chills down her spin when she heard a eerie song playing in the background. Only to later discover that the song was to torment her. A sign from the killer that she is being watch under close supervision. Of what better way to make a statement then by playing the song" Somebodys Watching Me" by Rockwell? Which is where all of the commotion begin? That sent Jill into a tailspin? As she begin to get paranoid about things in general. That the slightest little thing can set her off into an emotional wreck. The fact that she is being watch plays a huge role on her psyche. As she couldn't bare the thought of being prey upon by the unknown? Jill then begin to experience the effects of the song? By getting a glimpse of reality? As she begin to experience fear like no other? The fact that things just went haywire from then on. With the lights becoming a factor? Along with some whispers of her name being called in the distance. Which seem as if it was coming from all over. The fact that there were all sorts of different voices she was hearing. Telling her to "turn around" & by signaling her with noise saying" Over here"? Which terrified Jill, as she try to hold on to her sanity. As things became quite unbearable to withstand the amount of pressure she was under?

It seems as if the killer was mimicking her with that song playing in the background. Considering how hectic things have gotten, in result to all of this chaos. That basically says that Jill is a sitting duck of falling victim to her own fears? That the time has come to determine what fate has in store for her. Considering how well she can perceive the reality of distinguishing fact from fiction? That will decided the outcome to this conjunction? At this point? Jill seem lost for words. As she became disoriented about everything transpiring around her. Sending her world upside down by the many different responds she was getting from the conception. That made it difficult for Jill to come to terms with reality? Giving that the killer has Jill right where he wants her? By placing her in a very unusual position? Which is the scariest part of it all? As the whispers begin to get even closer. That at some point? She begin to experience what it exactly feels like to be terrify out of your mind. As she got the impression of what the" Torture Chamber" symbolize? That sent her jumping out of her skin when someone grab her shoulder from behind. While at the same time called her name. Which sort of put things in place of how to manipulate a person's mind with deception? By fluttering the mind with all sorts of delusions. To the point where everything seems misconstrued to the concept of it all? That things aren't always what they seem to be? Which seems to be the case as of now. Considering how Jill misinterpreted the lesson in reality? Which is that she is in a place where it is permitted to torture lost souls. By any means? Which is why she is made to suffer the consequences? Only this time! It seems as if she got lucky. That the hand that grab her was none other than Christian who was the one calling her name. Along with Marcus, who had to whisper to keep from being detected by the killers. The two of them couldn't be more happier to see each other in one piece.

That now is the time to make a break for the doors that would lead them out of this hellish nightmare. Which wasn't going to be easy according to Marcus? As he notify them that this particular section of the maze stretches a good distance. That is fill with all sorts of hidden surprise & booby traps. Which is design to torture souls. Which is something Jill witness a short while ago? However, it seems as if the map was going to make things a little easier on them. Considering that Marcus knew how to get pass this section quickly with the map. Even though, he couldn't predict what will happened, as a result? That he is just as well a newcomer like the rest of them. The only things he suggest to them? Is that they all stay close together? Jill on the other hand? Felt as if this whole thing is a setup to lure them in further. The fact that she couldn't get that song out of her head. As it constantly kept playing over & over inside of her mind. The fact that someone is watching them? Makes things much more creepy. Which made them put a little more pep in their step to avoid unwanted attention. It seems as if things were going smoothly, until they were interrupted by a woman's voice? That led to an horrifying scream. Which caught their attention? As this person was begging for someone to help her. It almost seem unreal of having to hear her desperate cry's for help? Immediately, Marcus advice them to not be fool by the out cry's of temptation. That it is all part of the show to draw in folks who are entertain by this sort of thing. That the best thing for them to do? Is ignore it & keep moving along to avoid any altercations with the killers. Who soul pupose is to manipulate them by getting them to follow the signs. Which didn't pan out all that well for Marcus & Christian. Who follow the path earlier only to find themselves at a crossroads? Which is something they regret doing?

It seems as if Jill couldn't shake off that song playing inside of her head. The fact that she just couldn't ignore hearing this person's plead for help? That she knew there would be consequences for their actions. If they don't look into what is going on around them. Which is a understatement to Christian & Marcus who consider this as some sort of trick to get them to fall for whatever. That their goal should be getting the hell out of this place. Jill felt as if it was suicide for them to keep going knowing that the killers are watching them. Which seems a bit unusual? The fact that the killers are just going to standby & let them escape. That for all she knows they could be headed down a treacherous path. That will determine the outcome of their fate according to the path they choose to follow. That they need to be more precise about the choices they make?

85

That the reality is that there is no way in hell they make it out of this place alive. Which is the statement the killers are trying to make by telling them to follow the signs? That all of the signs thrown their way had turn out disastous for them. Which tells the story of how they are marked for death. No matter how the cut go's, considering that it is pointless either way they look at it? Then from out of nowhere's! In comes running the woman who has been torture by the killer. The woman appear to be very frightened by what she experience. As her face seem scar from what appear to be burn marks. Of someone putting the works to her flesh. Damaging majority of her tissue that sustain third degree burns. Making her out as some sort of mutation with the severely burns. That disfigure her face all together which seems pretty far out. It was hard for the three of them to acknowledge the type of pain she was going through.

The woman then starts to panic when she realize that the killer had reappear from the shadows. Wearing one of the Faces of Death masks that symbolize fear. Which is one of the symptoms the woman is experiencing? The fact that she is in a state of shock? Which had the three of them concern about what has her all work up? When they too turn around & seen what the problem was? That had them all staring death in the face which was the least of their problems? The fact that their main focus is to stand guard against the perpetrator. In order to keep the woman safe along with themselves. Not realizing that there are two more dress in the Faces of Death attire. In which they wasn't expecting at the time. Who sort of caught them off guard by sneaking up on them from behind. While they were distracted by the appearance of the first killer. Which ended up with them being ambush by all three killers. Not knowing what direction the other two killers came from? Which was so surprising about this whole counterattack. The fact that they didn't see it coming? It seems as if the three of them were in the fight of their lives. Of trying to avoid be stab to death by the sudden attack, while the woman just stood there screaming uncontrollably? As it turns out that the joke was on the three of them considering how easily they are frightened? In which they are victims to the torture chamber. That this whole setup was to give them a run for their money. Considering that this is what it is all about? As it turns out? That the scars on the woman's face was nothing more than a job well done. Of using makeup to make it seem as if she was torture. Which was another sign from the killer that things aren't what they seem to be? Considering how they manage the game of distinguishing fact from fiction? That the idea of wearing the Faces of Death masks is to give into all of this speculation surrounding the history behind these three masks.

Which is the perfect formula to test out that theory that was suggested by a certain individual. That person of course being Mr. Shen who suggested the idea to them. Which raise a few eyebrows concerning the issue. Which alerted them that Mr. Shen is in the area? That most likely he is the one watching them. Planning out every detail, in order to manipulate the three of them. Which was nothing compare too what lies ahead according to the four actors. As they simply couldn't stress enough? That the mindgames behind some of these acts are horrendous? Which seems to be the theme behind the torture chamber, quoting it as" The Devil's favorite Playground"? That this is just a taste of things to come? Which kind of creeps the three of them out. Knowing that things are just going to get worse as they move along. It seems as if the four actors had to get back into character. To scare the next group that venture through these parts. Which had the three of them wondering what was the purpose behind that little issue. That it was obviously clear that the killer is up to something? Considering that there is always a point to be made from all of this? Which is the thing that worries them the most. No telling what Mr. Shen has up his sleeve. Just as Jill, Christian & Marcus begin to journey through the chamber. It seems as if they got distracted by one of the actors who reappear. Wearing the same Faces of Death mask as before? Only this time? It seem as if he was calling them back for some reason. By motioning his hand, as if he was telling them to come here? It was clear that the guy wanted something? So Marcus went over to see what the guy wanted? Figuring that maybe there was something else they fail to mention? While Jill & Christian stood by waiting on him to return? So that they can make their way through the torture chamber together in one piece.

CHAPTER 16

See No Evil

However, things didn't go according to plan as they were in for a rude awakening. That once Marcus reach the guy wearing the mask of pain? He seen that this person started to point his finger toward something behind him. That instantly! Made Marcus turn around to see what this person is trying to show him. Which allegedly turn out to be nothing, but total darkness? The fact that Marcus turn his back on a total stranger. Which was careless of him to do? Not at all expecting that it is the killer who fool them all by doing a double take of the mask. That was worn a second ago by someone else. Which resulted in death for Marcus who was stab multiple times in the back by the killer. Which goes to show the two of them that they can never be sure about certain appearance. Do to the fact that it may come off as being a deception? This however, made Christian very angry? As his emotions ran wild of wanting to get even by taking down his tormentor. Which is playing right into the killer's hands. Which is something the killer drives on? Making it very clear to Christian by tormenting him with the knife. Almost as if telling him to bring it on? It seems as if Christian had about just enough of being push around. The fact that he had it up to here, with the killer's shenanigans? The killer would then start to retreat when Christian came charging at him. Jill try to stop Christian before he end up in a body bag along with the others. It seems as though, she couldn't stop him in time? So she decided to go after him. Christian & Jill follow the killer deep in the chambers confinements. Where the two of them would lose site of the killer. Do to the lighting in the area that started to flicker very rapidly. Making it almost impossible to see what is going on around them. *The fact that Christian made a huge mistake by letting his emotions get the best of him.*

Which now puts him & Jill's life at risk all because he was too stubborn to listen. Which puts them in a very unfavorable position. Do to the fact that they have nothing to protect themselves if something was to happened? Not to mention? The fact that they are lost? Then suddenly, they begin to hear scraping sounds. As Christian took it to be some sort of sharp object, like a knife for instants? It was then when Christian got the impression that he is in way over his head. The fact that the killer continue to play mindgames with the both of them. By making it unpleasant for them to sustain any common ground. By using the flickering lights as cover to create an opening? That the time would soon presented itself when the killer made an unexpected sneak attack on Christian. However, Christian was well aware of the attack & manage to defend himself. Against the sudden swiftness of the killer who manage to get in one good swipe. That would send Christian reeling back toward Jill, but not without first snatching off the mask covering the face of the killer. Even though, they didn't see who it was? Do to the fact that it was accidental? Which was done out of the reaction of being stab. Which was the only thing he could grab a hold too? In order to try & keep his balance, as he was falling back toward Jill? The lighting also played a factor in not reveal who the person was behind the mask? At that point? Christian jump to his feet when he realize that the killer has no mask. He & Jill both went to find the killer. That there is no way they was going to let this opportunity of revealing who the killer is, slip through their fingers. The fact that they were right on the killer's tail, as that person desperately try to get away. Which is hard to do when there are stuff falling over. Which is a dead give away on where this person's headed?

Which would lead the two of them straight to the killer's where'a'bouts. In doing so, they manage to run into Jason who seem to have pop out of nowhere's at the last minute? Which was unexpected? Considering how he just appear momentarily after the killer completely vanishes? Which seems very ironic to Jill & Christian who begins to speculate what just occur. As they try to make sense of it all? That had the two of them interrogating Jason about what just happened? The fact that he suddenly turns up the second the mask gets pulled off? Which seems to them, as a way to cover his tracks. So that it doesn't connect him in any way of being the killer. Jason would then explain? That he had been lure here by the killer who advice him to follow the signs. In order to save the two of them from being killed. That it is all up to him whether they live or die depending on how well he can follow orders. That led to another conspiracy? Considering how he came up with the story of him being setup by the killer. Who has use him as bait to fool the two of them into believing that he is indeed the killer. Considering how Jill brought up the story of her getting a call from his cellphone. That labels him being the killer when they all thought that he was dead? Which seems like a simple explanation on Jason's part, as he begins to touch on that matter? Explaining that somehow he manage to drop his cellphone while being chase around by people wearing scary costume. Who he assume was the killer? That there was a good chance one of those individuals could of been the killer? Which would explain how the killer got a hold to his cellphone. Strangely enough, it all sounds legit to the two of them. Considering how Christian & Marcus have succumb to the temptation of being pawns in the killers plot, as well? That they too had been manipulated by this system. So he can kind of relate to what Jason is saying?

With that out of the way, the only things that remains is where did the killer disappear too? If it wasn't Jason? Who they were seriously considering at that point? Jason however, came up with the theory that maybe he scare whoever it was off? Considering the fact that this person was afraid to be discovered. Which couldn't come at a better time of labeling Jason as the suspect? Which is something Jill & Christian still couldn't understand? That by coincidence? Jason so happens to be in the area doing the time when the killer miraculously disappears. The moment when Christian pull the mask off the killer's face. Which had the two of them a bit concern about that issue? Which had them debating the issue of determining fact from fiction. Of a perception that seems a bit inconclusive? Considering how they were confuse by what they saw? That they must keep in mind that Jason & Eric seem mighty close as of late. Which all started that night in the galleria hall where they were first spotted together. That got them both thinking about how Jason was also consider as the killer around that time? Which is the straw that broke the camel's back? Which is the constellation behind the mystery that tells the story. Which is to get the two of them to follow the signs that will uncover the truth. Containing to the mystery that follows the reality concerning the issue with Jason. Which is to get them to see the truth of the matter before coming to terms with death. At that particular time? Jill & Christian begin to plan their escape. While Jason starts to strategize on how they go about making a move toward ending this?

While Jason back was trun to Christian? The opportunity had presented itself to make a break for it? The plan was for Jill to distract Jason long enough, until Christian can find something to knock him out with. Which was perfect? Considering that he won't be expecting it? The plan was working out perfectly, as Christian found a pipe to hit Jason over the head with.

    Everything went as plan as Christian took the pipe & knock it across Jason's head. That resulted to him being knock out from the blow. Christian then grab Jill's hand & started to make a bee line toward the exit. The only thing that stands in their way is not having any sense of direction on how to escape the haunted maze. Which is a real problem for them considering that there are two more killers on the loose. With the two of them being identify as Mr. Shen & Raymond Spencer as the other two killers. Which is something they must watch out for? To try & avoid those two people at all cost. Then it occur to Jill that maybe they should take a stand against the two of them. For all of the suffering they had to endure. Which seems like a bad idea to Christian who thought otherwise? However, Jill would go on to make a point that if they don't put an end to this now? Then they are as good as dead. Considering that the two of them won't stop until they are dead. Not to mention? That they know just as well who it is? That the only downside to this, is that they don't know what costume the two of them are in? Which is okay, Jill explain? That if the killers want them, then that's what they are going to get? As she made the suggestion that they find a costume to put on & blend in with the people around them. Who also has on costumes. So that it will be hard for the killers to detected the two of them. Long enough for them to escape the haunted maze. Where they can seek some help from the authorities. Which is a good thing considering that killers has no idea where they are? The fact that they got rid of one threat that has deceive them. Which was Jason? That now they can just wraps their way right out of here. Having to deal with no consequences, as a result to their actions?

    Christian seem a bit concern about that plan & suggested a whole new idea. That will benefit them better to sustain some common ground against a surprise attack from the killers. The fact that he is going to dress in a costume. While she look apart by staying casual. The plan was simple? According to Christian who told Jill to just follow his lead? The first thing they must do is to find a group of people to blend in with? Christian would then pay someone for their costume as the second part of his plan? Then they would be all set to carry out the rest of the plan. Which is to make the killer believe they got separated again. Considering how Jill is all alone with no sign of Christian anywhere's. Which is why she confine's herself to a group of people. Which is the disguise Christian needed to formulate his plan. The fact that he will look apart by wearing a costume. Which will throw off the killer into thinking that Jill is all alone. Which is where Christian's plan comes into full swing. By taking a page out of the killer's book. Which is to try & pull the wool over the killers eyes. By using the basic form of deception to catch the killers. Making Jill out as the bait, while Christian waits for the opportunity to present itself. Where he surprises the killers by catching them off guard. When they least expect it? That the whole dressing in a costume thing is to throw them off? Not realizing that this whole ordeal is a setup. Just in case the killers seem a bit tempting to cross their path. Which seem like a perfect plan to Jill who is all for it? The plan was now in place to make an attempt for the exit.

Jill had confine herself to a group of people, while Christian stood a good distance away from her. To ensure that nothing goes wrong. Christian try his best to look as casual as possible. In order to not make it obvious to the killers that he is around waiting on them to strike. Which is why Christian put some distance between Jill & himself? So far, Christian's plan is working out perfectly. Even though, there were a few intense moments in the torture chamber. That had some implications which kind of threw them off a bit. That almost jeopardize the mission. Causing, Christian to almost blow his cover? Meanwhile since then, Jill would receive a call from the killer. Who begins to torment her over the phone by constantly reminding her of the song" Somebody's Watching Me"? That the mindgames begins to play an issue on her psyche. As the killer starts to get inside of her head with all of the scary talk? Which involves the things that surrounds her. That being the torture chamber? Which is has it's own sadistic way of being sophisticated? The killer would use the chamber as his domain to scare Jill with all of the bad elements surrounding her. Jill had enough of being ridicule by the killer's mindgames & ended the call. That she knew then what the killer was trying to do? Which is to try & discourage her that she is in danger. To hopefully keep her from leaving. That all of the scary talk is just to manipulate her into believing something that isn't the case. The fact that she doesn't have to feel threaten by what the killer says? Considering how well their plan is going? That if the killer should attempt anything. Then it would be them who is in for a big surprise? As sad as it may seem, it was Christian who would get the surprise?

When his cover got blow the moment his phone started to ring. It seems as if the call was coming from the killer who took a page out of Christian's book? By calling his phone to see where he is at? Which is a spoiler alert for the two of them who is now at a stand still about what to do? However, Christian didn't answer the phone? Instead he grab Jill's hand & took off running in the chamber. In hopes that they can make it out in time before it is too late. Intensity fill the air? As they try to find their way out of the torture chamber. At that point? Things just begin to get crazier as they went further into the chamber. The fact that they had a difficult time of trying to manage through all of the craziness. That is transpiring all around them. That can send any person mad? Considering all of the stuff they have to go through? Which is just the beginning of their problems. The fact that there were all sorts of things being thrown in their face. By the many surprises that stood out as being a threat to them. Not knowing what is going to happened plays a huge role on the mind. That had them both stress out about the struggle they had to endure? Of figuring out how to go about finding their way out of this maze. Which is puzzling? Considering how it is structure. Which makes it that much difficult to sort out? Things have gotten so bad that Jill had to take a moment to gather her thoughts for a second. As she try explaining that all of this running doesn't help the cause. That they need to face their fears. Just as the killer "aka" Raymond Spencer suggested they do? That the time has come to face reality? Which seems to be right on the money. As Christian's phone begins to ring. Only this time? The call seems to be from Lisa's cellphone. Which is where things would get interesting?

CHAPTER 17

Redefining History

Christian rejoice to the fact that Lisa has regain consciousness again. As he past on the good news to Jill who wanted to know why does he seem so excited? The fact that he seem thrill to answer the phone for once? You couldn't imagine the feeling that came over him. The moment he heard Lisa's voice over the receiver. Which was so refreshing to Jill & Christian who thank god that she was alright. It was nice to know how much they consider her well being. That much is to be deserve of what she means to them. Which seems fine & dandy? However, there are more important things that she must attend too? Like addressing the issue containing to this mystery? That would shed some light on this entire case. Involving the Faces of Death murders that has been going on for sometime now? The fact that she has some information surrounding this case? That has led her to the killer who is pulling all of the strings. That got Jill & Christian thinking about Jason who they consider as the killer. Along with Raymond Spencer & Mr. Shen who is seeking vengeance against them for killing Eric? Considering how it is all starting to come together? However, it seems as if they were deceive by a lie? According to Lisa who inform them that this is all part of the game. Which is to blind them from the truth? Considering the fact that they are going to see what they want & not the conception that is reality. With that being the puppeteer who is controlling the issue. By manipulating every aspect of this entire situation? Making things out as an illusion to appear as it should? Which is where the links to the chain starts to connect? Lisa then starts to explain the issue concerning what brought this all on? Which all revolves around Jason & Eric who is accountable for these murders? Which had her wondering, where was Jason? That he too needs to hear this story she is about to lay on them.

They both explain what had happened to Jason as a result of him not being there with the two of them. Lisa then suggested that they go look for him immediately? Do to the circumstances that his life hangs in the balance. Which had Jill & Christian confuse on why should they help a killer? Which is why Lisa must tell them the story about what went on? That has started all of this mess in the first place. Lisa then begin to explain to the both of them about how it all got started. That involves a woman name Elizabeth Burton. Who was struck by a red camaro that belong to Eric Johnson. In the car with him was Jason & a couple of others who was out joy riding that night. That apparently they ran her over that night & then fled the scene for some reason? Without checking to see if she was alright. Which is a very serious issue for them. The fact that they fled the scene of a hit & run? Which was a mistake on their part of not realizing that Ms. Burton wasn't at all dead? In fact, she took it upon herself to get even with them. For leaving her on the side of the road. The fact that they left her for dead? Which is why to this day they are made to suffer the consequences for their actions. Along with those who are affiliated with them? Which is why she uses the Faces of Death masks? To exact her vengeance against those who left her for dead? By giving them a lesson they won't forget? Which all ended with them being killed in the process. Except for one? Who she has her sights set on. Which leaves Jason as the final piece to the puzzle? That had Jill asking? How can she be sure that it is Ms. Burton that is doing all of this? Lisa then replied that? The night of the incident. There were reports that her car was found wreck near the side of the road. However, there was not sign of her anywhere's. Which seems as no coincidence about her disappearance?

The fact of the matter is that as long as they remain in the haunted maze? The more they are at risk of being killed by Ms. Burton. Which is the reason why she is lying in a hospital bed now? Considering that her car crash was no accident by far? The fact that she almost paid the price for interfering in something that doesn't concern her? The fact that she kept knocking on the devils door & soon someone answer. That person being Ms. Burton? Who was aiming to killed her, once she discover the truth. Which seems rational at this point? That it was her this whole time pulling the strings behind the scenes. Planning her strategy to uphold the law into her own hands. Which she has been planning all along to get even with them by setting them up. By having them take the fall for the murders as a result to what they have done to her. Which is why it is up too the two of them to put an end to it? By stopping Ms.

Burton from killing Jason along with themselves for that matter. The fact that they all are marked for death by this curse. That if they are to survive this crisis? Then they must form a bond between the three of them to take Ms. Burton down for good? Which is the thing Lisa suggested they do? In the meanwhile, she is going to get the word out to every newscast across the nation about the Faces of Death murders case? That she is going to find her way out there. In order to give her statement to the news reporters that will be broadcasting the story live across the country. That it is her sworn duty to deliver the goods to the press. However, her first priorty is convincing the doctors to let her go? Which doesn't seem like no big ideal to her. Considering how she can smooth talk her way out of anything because of the person she is?

However, before letting Lisa go? Jill wanted to know the deal concerning the issue with Mr. Shen & Raymond Spencer? Of what role does the two of them play in all of this controversy. Lisa simply stated that Raymond Spencer was Eric Johnson's therapist. That his job was to help Eric cope with his problems. That while he was treating Eric it seems as if they form some kind of bond with one another. That a person of his stature is equip to handle cases such as Eric's? Which got him to realize that Eric was no killer. Despite what evidence was shown? The fact that he can detect a killer from certain stand points. Considering that he goes through these sort of things one day after another. With real criminals who commit murders. The fact that he is professionally train to handle these sort of issues. That according to his philosophy these issues doesn't apply to Eric? That got Lisa wondering if it was him who help Eric escape from the mental hospital that night? The fact that Raymond did all he could to help Eric. Which is why he is made to suffer the consequences for his actions? Raymond then would go as far as to join forces with Mr. Shen who is an expert on the three Faces of Death masks. The fact that Mr. Shen is the spokesperson for the history behind the three masks. In fact, he study the masks quite often, as susposed to how it is link to the halloween murders? So the two of them came up with the plan to created the House of Horrors for this year's fright'tober fest. That the haunted maze was design to catch the killer. That somehow they would have to lure the killer there? Which is where the three of them come in? Which got Jill & Christian thinking that it wasn't by coincidence Jason got those three free tickets. The fact that they was baited into doing this by Raymond & Mr. Shen who use reverse psychology on them.

By offering free tickets to Jason on a job well done of advertising the upcoming event. While they were bribe into doing this with a little persuasion from Raymond Spencer. Who told them to face their fears? That for some reason the killer manage to always stay two steps ahead of them. That instead of being effective? They only manage to fall victim to their own plan? Which is demoralizing to say the least? Which made Christian realize that the person Ms. Burton refer to as being the killer amongst them. Wasn't Jill, it was Jason? Which points out the obivous about certain clues that was given? Like for instant, I know your secret? Which was written in cold blood at last year's halloween bash. That took place in the woods at Jason's father cabin. The idea was brought to Jill's attention that Lisa should send them a picture of Ms. Burton. Considering that they have no knowledge of what she looks like? Which will help them to know who to look out for? Just in case they run into her by some reason. It seems as if they were out of lucky at this point? Considering that there was no picture of her to send? Do to the fact that she took all of the evidence away the night of the accident? Which is why Lisa must prove her case in some other way. Which is why she is on her way down there now to explain everything? The fact that now they are back to square one of not knowing who the killer is? Considering that they have no knowledge on what she looks like nor the mask she has on? Which is nerve wrecking of knowing the name of the person that is doing all of this? Only to discover that they have nothing else to go along with it? Which stands out in their mind as being rob to a certain extent?

Jill & Christian then wrap up their conversation with Lisa so that they can go look for Jason. It seems as if there are some unfinished business they need to attend too? As far as them getting to Jason in time before the killer does? Not to mention? The fact that they have their work cut out for them as of seeking out the killer Ms. Burton? Who they have no idea what she looks like? Which makes things difficult on their end. Then to make matters worse is that they must retrace their steps by going back into the torture chamber. To search for Jason? Which was something they didn't care to do? Considering all that they went through while they was in there the first time. The fact that they are going to have to relive the horror that torments them. Which by the way isn't going to be easy to do? Considering all of the hidden surprises that they didn't come across the first time. Being that they took a different route other than the one they are on? Being that it is a maze & all? Which pretty seems all the same except for some minor changes that separates the venue. Things just seem disheartening on how the situation turn from bad to worse. As they had to *suffer the effects of the torture chamber. Despite how badly things are going. They still wasn't going to abandon their friend in his time of need. While in search for Jason? They decided to play it safe by staying close to people who are in a group. Until, they can figure out what to do? Considering the situation with Jason? The fact that how are they going to know that this isn't a trap to lure them straight toward the killer. That there's a good chance she is waiting on them to show up.*

Even though, it's a risk they would have to take considering that it's their only option? Considering how their lives also hangs in the balance. Which made them decide to face their fears by confronting their tormentor? Which seems like the rational thing to do? If they are to rid themselves from this curse once & for all. Which will put an end to all of the senseless killings that is taking place. After all, what do they have to lose? Based on the fact that it's either going to be them or her who walks out of this maze alive? Which seems like the only outcome on how things would turn out. That the only way out of the maze is through the killer who is standing in their way. Which doesn't seem like a big deal if that's what it takes for them to escape, then so be it? However, they still would have to be careful about the people that surrounds them. Considering that the jury is still out on the fact that they have no clue on what this person looks like. Then to make it worse? Not knowing the costume she will appear in? Which make things harder for the two of them to continue the search for Jason. Who is probably dead somewhere's according to the both of them. That by the time they get to him, it maybe already too late. Which is the thing that worries them the most? As they try to figure out which way to go in the maze? In order to get to the spot where they left him lying unconscious. It seems as if their self conscious mind has been disrupted by other distractions. Which seems to have affected their way of thinking. The fact that they seem lost & was unable to gather their bearing. Considering how it is all starting to take it's toll on them. Making them lose their composure by how intimidating this place can overwhelm a person's mind. By all of the antics that surrounds them. Which is the mindgames that being played on them by the killer.

Who is doing so, without so much effort to say the least? That the effects of the chamber is working on the behalf of the killer. Which is why Marcus wanted to avoid this place at all cost? Considering that everything about this place just seem depressing to them. However, it wasn't long from now, when they finally reach the area where Jason was? To their surprise? They discover that there was no Jason anywhere's to be found? Only a mask that symbolize fear? Which represents the torture chamber. At that point? Jill brust into tears considering the fact that she regrets taking him for granted doing these past years. Christian try to consoled her the best way that he could? To try & get her to see that just because Jason is not here? Doesn't mean that he is dead? That the only way to be sure, is to locate him? That he is in here somewhere's probably wandering around. The fact that he has no idea about what is going on? Which is sad about this whole thing? The fact that he is responsible for all of this? Which is where it all ends with him. Which is why they must get to Jason, in order to warn him of the danger headed his way. If he is alive? Which is the question that is weighing heavily on their minds as of now? The fact that Ms. Burton might be playing games with them. By giving the two of them the run arounds to look for Jason who is probably dead? Which is something they must know for sure. Before they start planning their escape? Jill knew that the more time they spent in the torture chamber. The more likely they will suffer the consequences for their actions. Which gives Ms. Burton more than enough time to carry out her plans. Which seems reasonable for Christian who agree with Jill to start planning their get away. That no matter how the cut goes? She still was going to come after them for matter what? So all that is left is to confront her & hope for the best? Considering that she wouldn't get away with it? Do to the fact that Lisa is on to her.

CHAPTER 18

The Past has Return

That if for some reason they don't make it out of the maze alive? Justices will still prevail when the killer Ms. Burton is finally capture. Once the word gets out that she is the one who is responsible for the halloween murders? Even though, Jill & Christian didn't have their hearts set on dying. Which was a statement just in case by chance things pan out that way. That they are going to confront their greatest fear of all? Which is to play this thing all the way down to the wire. Which will eventually lead them to the killer? Which will be the final act in the closing moments. That will determine the outcome of the ending results? Which will play itself out before the curtain go's up on this entire venue. Which is how it is all shaping up? That no matter how they try to downplay it? The two of them must of known that it would end up this way? With them facing uncertainty death? Do to the concept that they have nothing to rely on? Execpt the fact that they know her name & the reason for her doing this? Which leaves very little lead way on who they should be watching out for? Considering the fact that Ms. Burton is still a threat to them, even without the mask? Do to the fact that they not know who she is? Which is hard for them to try & come up with a plan. Considering what's at stake? Of not knowing what they are up against? Which seems very uncommon? Based on the reality that they are facing certain death. Of rushing into a situation, not knowing the percussions behind them. Which is the thing that worries the two of them concerning the issue with the uncertainties. The fact that they are not going to know when it's coming, but rest to sure? They are going to be on the look out for anything unusual. That their main focus will be escaping the maze.

That way, they can almost anticipate when the killer will strike the closer they get to the exit. Which is the perfect plan of predicting when the killer would strike? Which will make them more aware of a surprise attack. Do to the fact that they will be expecting it? The two of them then begin to make their way through the torture chamber. In search, for the exit that would relieve them of the stress of being hunted. That once they are outside, then things would be okay? Even though, they would still be at risk? Considering that Ms. Burton can blend in with the people around her. By wearing a mask once she too exit the maze. Which is probably the alternative in what she is planning on doing? Which is to make it seems as if she is waiting on the two them somewhere's in the maze. When actually she is probably waiting on the outside of the maze. Waiting on them to exit the perimeter. So that she can sneak up behind them when they least expected it? Which could be the nail in the coffin that claims both of their lives. Which was something Christian pick up on as a possibility? The fact that they can never tell what Ms. Burton has up her sleeve? Which is the one thing they mustn't do? Which is underestimate how deviant she can be? That they must be careful not to fall victim to her scheme. That it is critcal that they remain relevant to the cause & not be fool by what they see? Strangely enough? Things haven't gone the way they thought it would? That while, they search for a way out of the chamber. They manage to run into Jason who they spotted walking around. With his hand planted on the back of his head where he was struck with the iron pipe by Christian. It seems as though, he was sort of in a daze from the blow he suffer? Christian & Jill both rush to his aid, in hopes that he didn't sustain any bad injuries to his head. However, he did seem a bit bang up, but other than that, he seem okay? Although, Jason had no knowledge about what happened to him?

That the last thing he remember is talking to Jill about escaping the maze. Then all of a sudden everything just went black & that he awoke to find himself lying face first in the dirt. With people standing around him? Asking him, if he was okay? Only to discover that the two of them were gone? Which had him thinking the worse case scenario at that point? That something bad must have happened to the two of them. Surely Christian would explain what took place. As he gave Jason a heart felt apology about the misunderstanding? Surely there was no hard feeling between the two of them. As they both put their differents aside by fist bumping each other. Now that they put this little incident behind them. They can move on to other important things like the issue concerning Jason? They told him, that there are things he needs to know about the halloween murders. Which have to deal with him & Eric? At that point? Jason seem a bit concern on what was about to come up? The fact that they can see it in his eyes that he was hiding something? They then explain the situation to him about what is going on? According to Lisa's story about the incident that involves him & Eric. Hitting a lady with Eric's red camaro? Jason then confesses to the allegation that the story is true. That it was the thing that has been eating away at him for all these years. Not knowing that he is the cause for all of this chaos? Still & all, Jill & Christian wanted to know the truth about what happened that night? Jason felt oblige to come forward with the truth? Feeling as though, he owe them that much. Considering all that they went through because of his negligence of failing to accept responsibility for what he has done. That he wasn't going to get any sympathy from the two of them. Considering that what they did was wrong on all levels. That there is no excuse for what they did to her, the way that they did?

Even though, it doesn't give her a right to retaliate, as a way to get back at them? Which resulted in death for so many people who had nothing to do with it? All because she wanted to send a message to them. That what goes around, comes right back around? Which is why Jason is in the predicament he is in? That he & his friends are the blame for all of this? As Jason begin explaining his side of the story. About what transpire that night? Jason told them that the night of the accident he & couple of his buddies decided to take a ride to his father's cabin. The same cabin they were at last year doing halloween? That they were suposed to meet a couple of friends there. That he hasn't seen since his childhood. That they all were going to meet up at the cabin. At that time? Jason didn't know Eric all that well? That he just met Eric through a mutual friend that night in a bar. Who wanted to come along for the ride. It seems as though, Jason didn't have enough room in his car for everyone. So they decided to go in Eric's camaro since it had more space to fit everyone. Considering that it was just the four of them anyway? It seem very fitting that Eric wanted to show off his new ride by showcasing it's speed. Even though, he wasn't suposed to drive it? Considering that he was still on probation doing that time. Do to the fact that he was driving on a suspended license. Still in all? He manage to sneak it out that night while his mother was asleep? Despite the warnings that it is his last strike, but what else can you expect from a teenager. Who is free to do whatever the night of your graduation. The fact that Eric wanted to celebrate with his friends. Which involve a lot of drinking that night.

Considering how they all manage to sneak in the bar that night. By making false ID's for themselves? Even though, they didn't look their age which kind of help their situation a bit.

Which led them to explore the open road to Jason's father's cabin? The fact that they all seem wild & disorderly up to this point? As they blast the radio to it's maximum to express how good life is? That had them feeling good despite the fact that alcohol played a major role on how they were behaving. That eventually led to the accident? Considering how it all happened so fast? That Ms. Burton came out of nowhere's? Considering how she came stumbling out in front of the car? That it was so sudden? That Eric couldn't avoid her at the rate he was going? Which turn disastrous within that split second? Jason would go on to say that they all was in a state of shock by what just happened? As emotions ran high to the point where they started to panic? That study shows that people who have panick attacks doesn't fold well under pressure? With them being under the influence doesn't help the situation either. The fact that their thought process is useless? That help them make the wrong decision which is something they later regret doing? The fact that Eric was so concern about how this could affect his life. That this is his final strike? That there was no way he was going to jail, under no circumstances? Which got them all bickering over the matter. That not one of them went over to check on Ms. Burton which was their mistake. Figuring that she was dead? At that point? They all seem scare about the consequences they will have to face for killing someone. Which is all they could think of, at that point? Afraid that someone might drive up on them & discovers that they hit somebody. Yet alone, that they are under the influence which will make matters worse when the police arrive on the scene. The fact that they will be charge with manslaughter? Which was a chance they wasn't willing to take.

So they got back into the car & drove off to the cabin to think this thing over. However, once they reach the cabin tempers started to flare between the four of them. As they bicker the whole nine yards about who's to blame for all of this? Which seems pointless? Considering that none of them wanted to take responsibility for what they have done? The fact that now, they are looking at a hit & run added on to the charges. Which didn't make any sense to Christian & Jill? Who thought mighty less of Jason? Considering how could he be so stupid to just leave the scene of the crime like that? Considering that he should of known the consequences for leaving the crime scene. Jason try to explain the reason for him leaving. Which is that they was going to leave him stuck out in the cold. All because the three of them had a rap sheets from previous incidents. That has to deal with reckless driving. Which was consider as minor compare to this incident? Which is the thing Jason try to get the two of them to see. Which is that he had no other choice, but to get in the car with them. Being that it was during the middle of the night when the whether was at it's worse. That he didn't want to take the chance of freezing to death waiting on someone to come through with a car. Which was inexcusable to say the least. According to Jill & Christian who saw it as no excuse for him leaving. Considering how can he be so selfish to think only of himself. When there is a person in need of some medical attention. Which is why they can see the reason behind Ms. Burton actions toward them? Considering how they just left her there to die.

That there is no excuse for him leaving her out there alone in the cold. All because his friends had a record & that he didn't want to rat them out to the police? That because of his actions? He is made to suffer the consequences for those actions. That because of his negligence others had to suffer the consequences for his mistake. Including the two of them who Ms. Burton now has her sights on? Jill despise Jason for what he has done. The fact that she couldn't look at him anymore. Jason would go on to say that while the four of them were in the cabin. They made a pact that this little incident stay between the four of them. That it would be their little secret? Eric told them not to worry about it? Because he was going to take care of it? Still to this day? Jason has no idea how Eric manage to cover it up? Which is a understatement? Considering that all Eric manage to do? Is make matters worse by trying to cover it up. As Christian try to get Jason to see the bigger picture that the secret is killing them? That she isn't going to stop at nothing, until they are all dead. The fact that they try to cover it all up by brushing it off? As if nothing happened? Makes the road to redemption all the more sweeter. The fact that the past has caught up with them & now? They must suffer the consequences for what they did? That she is only doing what should of been done the first time around. Which is for them to take the rap for the attempted murder. That they try to get away with it by trying to cover it up & failed miserably? That the way things stand as of now? There is nothing Jason can do to make things right again? Which is something he will have to live with for the rest of his life.

Lucky for him, Lisa made it apparent that Ms. Burton is the killer? Which had them thinking that since her cover has been blow. Then the only thing left

in their direction. As the voices begin to get closer to them. Doing the time when the lights begin to cut off? Which alerted Jill & Jason that it was time to go? As they all took off running toward the next stage in the torture chamber. That by the lights going off the way it did made it clear that they was no longer in the first stage of the torture chamber. As that section went completely dark? That much was clear. However, they didn't know what to make of the voices that they heard calling their names? Which doesn't seem like it was part of the show? Which by the way dissipated once they enter through the gates. Of the second stage of the torture chamber. Which almost seems as if they were force into this situation. Do to a little persuasion of the mind from the voices calling in the distance. Which is uncertain on whether it was the killer or someone else calling their names? That time would soon tell just what's in store for the three of them. That will define the odds of what is reality? Which is something they now have to face? Based on the eerie feeling they have about this particular stage of the chamber. That sets apart from anything they have seen so far? The fact that it is cold & dark with the conception of an old abandon building. That just have that scary feel to it? Of something bad happening within the matter of minutes. The type of building that has all sorts of weird & scary sounds to it. That makes a person just wanted cringe with fear when they hear the slightest noise? A place where everything is boarded up & the floor squeaks when you walk across it?

If that's not terrifying enough? Then just think about the sudden stillness this place has? The fact that it is too quiet, makes it that much more scarier. The three of them decided to stick close together. Afraid of what they may incounter along the way? The fact that they couldn't get those voices out of their heads. Which plays a significant role on their thought process? That they are in for a big surprise? Which is something they can expect to happened? Even though, they couldn't speculate when it would occur? That timing is everything? According to how well it is choreograph. Which would determine how people will react to such a thing. When something unexpected happens? Which is the thrill of it all? The fact that they won't see it coming? Which is the thing that sends chills down their spine. Just thinking about it? The fact that someone would dare mock them by playing mindgames with them. Considering that they can hear someone tagging along behind them. That everytime they stop to make sure no one is following them. It seems as if this person would also pause & continue to walking along with them. Repeating the process time & time again? Which got them thinking about one person who they suspect is doing all of this? At one point? It seems as if someone was draging themselves across the floor. Like some sort of corpse? Which got the three of them all work up? About what it is, that is sliding across the floor like that? Which had them running through the chamber toward an area? Where they found themselves surrounded by old fashion wooden coffins? Which is puzzling to them of what to make of it? A place that is fitting for the undead to rise up from the grave.

Which seems very unusual considering how it is portray that has the three of them concern over the matter. The fact that they didn't know what to make of it all? Considering how the coffins were standing upright against the wall. It would seem as if nothing good can come from this? By their standards? Considering that they are surrounded by coffins. Which isn't the thing that concerns them. The fact that what's inside of the coffins lies the problem. As they didn't put anything past the killer who excel at these sort of things? That the torture chamber is the perfect hunting ground for Ms. Burton. To cause all sorts of conflict within the different stages of the chamber. However, nothing would be more frightening? Then when the only two doors in the room slam shut. Which scare the bejesus out of them. Considering that they wasn't expecting that to happened? No matter how hard they try to open the doors, it wouldn't budge an inch. Which is the worse thing possible to imagine? The fact that they are trap in a room full of coffins, not knowing what awaits them on the inside. Which is the thing that is so terrifying about this whole situation. Which left them with only one option? That is to search the perimeter for any hidden latch in the compartment of this room. That will unlock the doors to this room? Which always seems to be the case in these sort of situation. While searching the room for some kind of trigger mechanism that will open the doors. Christian came up with a theory of his own. That he is willing to bet his last dollar that the key to opening these two doors. Lies within one of these coffins? That by chance if they open the right coffin than the doors will open? However, what's the chance of something bad happening if they open the wrong one? Which is the the thing that worries Jill & Jason about the implications that may have some repercussions, as a result.

That one by one they begin to discover the truth about what is going on with the coffins? That as they open each coffin it seems as if a bit of the past is rediscovered? By having to relive those terrifying moment from the previous years. Of having to stare into the face of famous slashers from the movies.

That was use in previous killings from the past. Like the ghostface costume & the Micheal Myers attire or the slicker outfit from" I know what you did last summer"? That every slasher costume that was ever use? Is now, starting to reemerge inside of each one of these coffins? Until, it led up to the last costume the killer wore? Which was the dreadful baby killer getup from the horror movie" Valentine"? Which leaves the question about what famous slasher Ms. Burton is now impersonating? Although, it is all being perceived as a countdown of each costume the killer has wore. Which now leads to only three undiscovered coffins? That were missing three costumes? Although, all of the rest of costumes that was place inside of the coffins? Seem unreal, to the point where the three of them have mistaken them to be manikins. As so they thought? That once they turn their backs toward the open coffins. The opportunity was in place for the unfortunate turn of events to occur? When the people inside of the coffins went on the offensive by impersonating the famous slashers from the movies. Grabbing a hold to all three of them? Pulling them back toward the coffins so that they couldn't escape. As it turns out? That these so called mannequins dress up in famous killers attire. Were real people after all? Deep down the three of them knew that one of these impersonators was indeed Ms. Burton. The thing is? That they didn't know what killer she was impersonating? Which is a hard thing for them to distinguish fact from fiction. When they seen a band of people dress in scary costumes from the movies. Charge at them with all sorts of weapons that defines the killer?

Like the killer Jason voorhees who carries around a machete or leatherface who has a chainsaw? Which is the thing that seem so terrifying to them? The fact that either one of these people could be Ms. Burton. Somehow, Jason manage to break free from one of the killers grib & was able to render his friends free as well. They then was able to get the door to open as they spilled their way out into the hallways of the chamber. Although, the people dress as killers. Took a much different approach by spreading out within the chamber's confinements. Circling around the three of them in the dark trenches. As they were startled by the many different footsteps prancing around them. With the addition of adding insult to injury by taunting them with the sounds of terror. With the running of the chainsaw & the sounds of sharping knifes. Which plays as a gimmick for what's to come? As they could hear that same person calling out to them. The same as before? When that certain someone begins whispering their names. Which had Jill freaking out? Considering all that is going on right now? To the point where she couldn't take it anymore? As she separated herself from Jason & Christian? Where she found herself pinned against the wall by a show of hands. That grab a hold to her when she back into an opening in a doorway. That was somewhat broaded up when the hands reach out to grab her. Although, it was all part of the show? Reality then begins to kick in, as the perception becomes more clear by the minute. Of determining what the torture chamber is truly about? Jill seem terrify by the sudden encounter she endure with the situation involving her being grab by a show of hands. That cause her to reacted in such a way? That had her screaming uncontrollably? Over something that seems a little ridiculous to any normal person. Who is unaware that their is a psycho running around these parts? Who thinks that this is all part of the show? When the truth of the matter is that they see what they want to see? That they can expect these sort of things to occur inside of a haunted maze.

Which is the thing that has sidetrack them all from what's really going on? The fact that the killer known as "Ms. Burton" is using the haunted maze as a certify resource? To carry out her plans in a way where no one would suspect a thing. Which makes it tough on the three of them to get people to see what is really going on? However, Jill manage to break free from the many hands that had her pinned against the wall. With a little assistant from Jason & Christian who pull her away in time. Before the killer got there to take full advantage of the situation. Do to the fact that Jill had her hands full at the time. Which would have been easy pickins for the killer. Even though, they are not out of the woods yet? Being that they still have multiple of famous killers from the past in their midst. That it is going to be difficult to determine which of them is Ms. Burton. Who they suspect is somewhere's hiding in the shadows waiting for the opportunity to present itself? Which makes matters worse considering that they don't know which famous slasher she is impersonating? Not to mention? That they need to be on the look out for any other surprises. Considering that this whole setup could be just a distraction to take the three of them by surprise. With a whole new appearance of some sort to throw them off? Just like before when Marcus was killed? No telling what kind of costumes that was missing from those remaining three coffins? That had them wondering which three famous slashers is up for the running. As they try to imagine what horrifying killers they would have to put up with next? That were missing from those *three coffins. Despite the that there are famous killers all around them that they must account for?*

Timing is everything according to how to set a mark? Which was the perfect time to sent out a message to Jill's cellphone. From the killer Ms. Burton who sent her a text message from Jason's cellphone saying" What is their favorite scary movie of all times"? Which to them is consider as an insult to their intelligence. That she would dare mock them with an variety of scary costumes from the slashers flims. The fact that Ms. Burton wanted to make a statement to the three of them. That their greatest fear of all is about to get much more terrifying? Not wanting to back down? Jill sent out a message of her own to Jason's cellphone that is in the sole possession of the killer. That stated" She know who this person is"? That justice will prevail when the truth comes out? At that point? Jill waited for a responds from the killer. As it turns out? There wasn't any? Which means that they got Ms. Burton's attention with that statement that they are on to her. That maybe she will back down now? Considering that the game is over. On the other hand? She may feel that if she go's down, then she is going to take the three of them along with her. Meaning that she will take whatever measures to make sure they don't walk out of this place alive. Which is the thing they were unsure about? Considering how Ms. Burton would go about things now that they know who she is? However, the negative thing about it? Is that they don't know what she looks like? Which is the only thing that stands in their way. Seems as though, the worse as yet to come. As they still have to sort out this mess with the different killers. Not to mention? Entering the third stage of the torture chamber. Where things are sure to get even more scarier. Which is something they must prepare themselves for? If they are to make it out of this place alive. However, time will tell if Ms. Burton is true to her word that vengeance is substantial, as susposed to her running away.

CHAPTER 20

Death is Calling

In the meanwhile, Jill & her two comrades were left to face adversity. When the people who are impersonating famous slashers from the movies. All begin to retreat, in order to hide themselves from Jill & her two buddies? In a game better known as" The Missing Link"? Which is part of the program that was shown on the alert montior. That even though this is all stage as part of the show? They knew that this will be the defining moment in how the game is to be decided? The fact that this game is based around finding who the killer is? Which is right up their alley? Which is sort of related to the board game clue? Where the audience must decide who amongst the people that is impersonating famous slashers from the movies is the real killer. Not knowing that this is actual going on? Which is the thing that is painful to Jill & her two friends. The fact that people are playing right into the killer's hand. By thinking that this is some sort of joke? When in reality? This is a serious matter for the three of them. The game is center around a bunch of trivia questions that relys on fact & fiction clues. That these clues can lead them to the truth behind the mystery killer. Or misguided them to the wrong killer. Which all depends on what road they are willing to go down. Based on the clues they choose to follow? That will decide the outcome to this little game. That the object of the game is to find the missing link to the puzzle. Which will lead them to the killer based on how well they can piece together the missing links of the puzzle. That there will be two options to choose from. One being fact while the other is fiction? Considering that they must choose wisely on the choices they make. Which seems to be the coming out party for Ms. Burton who loves to play games with people's minds.

However, it seems as if they were up for the challenge. Considering that they have no other choice, but to go along with what's going on?

If they want to get to the bottom of all this conspiracy about who is she? Something Jason is looking forward too, in order to come to terms with his past. In hopes that they can bury the hatchet between the two of them. Which seems very unlikely at this point? The idea of this game is to torture the three of them with the haunting of famous slashers from the past. They had to endure doing these past years of having to face it all over again? That tells the story about each encounter they had with each of these costumes. That now, they would have to be on guard about each person they come across. Who is impersonating slashers from the movies. Considering that one of them could indeed be Ms. Burton? Despite the appearance of how things are beginning to take form. They must not be fool by what they see? That they knew how things can be misinterpret by the wrong perception. Which makes it that much difficult for them to stay on track. For all they know? This could be a setup to get them in a position. Where the odds are stack against them to wore off any unexpected sneak attack by the killer. Who is using every resource to her advantage. By following these clues they manage to run into a few surprises along the way. That had them all afraid of what they may encounter next. Seems as though, things just keep getting worse as they move far into the chamber. They had numerous close calls, everytime they came across someone wearing a slasher costume. That resembles the one's from their past encounters. Including the one's from tonight? The fact that it seem so realistic to the point where they felt the same way as those victims in the movies. However, this was no movie? As the intensity was too overwhelming to think that this is just a fantasy. That they would be starring in their own real life horror movie with the killers they grew up watching on television. Which is the thing that is so scary about this whole ordeal? Considering that this is the reality they have to face?

The fact that nothing compares to what they have face tonight? Considering how things just turn hectic inside of the second stage of the torture chamber. Which makes them wonder about the third & final stage of the chamber. Of what sets the two stages apart from one another which is the question they must ask themselves. Figuring that it can't get much worse than this? However, the way things are going as of now? They wasn't sure that they would make it to the final stage if this keeps up? The fact that death is calling out to them? With the many distractions of famous killers being thrown their way. Considering how it seem almost impossible to get through this situation without being targeted by the killer. Which is the question? That which one of the impersonators wearing a costume is Ms. Burton? Which was something they couldn't figure out? Of why she hasn't try to kill one of them yet? Considering that there were moments where she could of easily slip in unnoticed. When they weren't paying attention? Considering that their main focus was on something other than what they were expecting? Which is the costumes from halloween's past? When there are other scary costumes in the area that needs to be observe by the three of them. However, there was still questions about the costumes that were missing from the three coffins. Which is another concern that they must worry about? The fact that Ms. Burton could be wearing a new costume they know nothing about? Which is the conflict they have to put up with? Then Christian came up with a theory based on the clues they have gather. That would sum up the situation with the three empty coffins? The fact that all of the coffins they had open up? Was famous slashers costumes from the past? Leading up to tonight's three costumes the killer Ms. Burton has worn? Which leaves out three other costumes that was worn continuously throughout the course of these murders? That the three costumes that was missing from those three coffins?

Was none other than the three Faces of Death masks that is this town's landmark for this years halloween extravaganza? Which is also the missing link to this game. The only problem is trying to figure out which one of the three masks is Ms. Burton hiding under? Yet alone? Trying to locate the three masks in the midst of all this chaos surrounding them. The fact that they would have to use their better judgement. In order to seek out Ms. Burton who's identity still remains a mystery to them. That the only thing they can go by? Is that she is a woman dress in one of the face of death attire. Which was the direction they choose to follow. According to the evidence they receive, as being the facts of determining the games persona? However, they didn't leave out the possibility of being in denial. When it comes to the head games that is misleading. About certain standards of the game that can change instantly? Leading them to believe something that is not the case. That for all they know? Ms. Burton could be dress in some other scary costume. Other than the one they believe she is wearing. Which is one of the three faces of death costumes. That if they learn anything from all of this? Is that, they need to be aware of everything that crosses their path. That there is no room for margin of error on their part. Considering that this is a life or death situation? Which is the thing that has them all concern? About trying to locate a needle in a haystack? Which seems almost impossible to do, when there are impersonators at every corner of the chamber. Which makes things harder on the three of them to determine the differents between fact from fiction? Then it suddenly occur to Jason that things aren't as bad as they seem? As he came up with a brillant plan to catch Ms. Burton. When she least expects it? That had Jill & Christian tipping their hats off to him on a well thought out plan. Once Jason hip them to what he was doing, the moment he reach for Jill's cellphone. That there was no way she was going to give them the slip this time around?

The plan was simple to follow, if they go about it the right way. Jason plan is to track down his cellphone by using Jill's phone in order to trace it to Ms. Burton. In hopes, that she still has his phone in her possession. That he is going to use the tracker in Jill's cellphone to locate his phone. Which will lead them to the killer Ms. Burton, if they are lucky? Which seems like a good idea compare to none at all? Which seems like their best bet to hunt her down for once? That for once? There plan begin to look up. As the tracker on Jill's phone begin to anticipate the movement of Jason's phone. They then begin to follow the signal to where Jason's phone is located? Which wasn't that far off from where they were. That had the three of them guessing that Ms. Burton stood waiting in the shadows. For them to come through so that she can sneak up on them unexpectedly. Which is something they anticipated from the start. However, they manage to seek her out & lock in on her position. Not realizing that the three of them are sneaking up on her unexpectedly? Oh' how the tables has turn in their favor? That the time has finally come to take full control of this situation. By putting an end to this conspiracy once & for all? That finally, they can catch the one responsible for all of these murders. That their friends death won't be in vain. Even though, they didn't deserve it, to begin with? However, there seems to be flaw in Jason's plan? The fact that they don't want to seem to conspicuous? By looking around the chamber to see what costume she has on? Which would be a dead give away. That somehow they would have to look a part, which gave Christian the idea that they should wear a disguise? That in order to pull this off? They need to take a page out of the killer's book & put on a disguise. To shield themselves from being detected by Ms. Burton. Jason did a little negotiating with a couple of people. In order to borrow their costumes for a couple of minutes. It seems as if their plan is now in full swing of capturing the killer?

That now is the time to strike when the killer has her guard down. The fact that she won't be expecting this to occur? As they finally reach the area where Jason's phone seems to be located. The only thing for them to do? Is to follow the signal to the spot where Jason's phone is? At first, they thought that the killer may have gotten rid of the phone. However, that would soon change when they started to get closer to the spot where the phone was located? Which seems to be coming from a person wearing a Michael Myers costume? Which at that point seem kind of unusual? Considering how Jason's plan came through for them after all? The fact that they can tell by looking at this person's body language. That this person is up to something? Which got them thinking about one person that comes to mind. All that is left for them to do? Is try & figure out how to approach the situation. That just as they suspected? Ms. Burton doesn't have a clue about what is going on? They then begin to strategize how to take her down. Without anyone getting hurt in the process. Which didn't require a lot of thinking considering that she has no knowledge. About what they have done? That it would be easy for them to just walk up behind her unexpectedly & grab a hold to her. Considering that they too have on disguises. Just like the killer, Jason waited for the opportunity to present itself? As the three of them begin to close in on her. They then begin to take their place in the attempt to catch her. As they form a circle around her to keep her from getting away? Just as they got into positon the time was now to seize the moment. As they all make the attempt to grab her before she could figure out what was going on? They manage to catch her. Even though, she seem a bit strong when they try to get a hold to her. It seems as if their plan work out beautifully? As they recovered Jason's cellphone that was in the killer's possession. However, things took a turn for the worse when Christian pull off the Michael Myers mask?

As it turns out that when Christian pull off the mask a bit of confusion grew on their faces. When they discover that the person behind the mask wasn't Ms. Burton? Instead, it was a young man impersonating the michael myers character. Which seems innocent enough? Based on his reaction when they caught him by surprise. Which was something this young man wasn't expecting to happened? However, there were questions about how he ended up with Jason's phone. The young man told them that he had found it? Which is understandable considering that the killer had no use for it? Based on the fact that they know who she is? Which brings up another question about why he seem so suspicious? The young man then applied, that he was playing a game with a couple of friends. The three of them felt as if they were total losers. By entertaining this stupidity of a game. As they gave an sincere apology to the young man for giving him a hard time. That once again? They were manipulated by the killer's mindgames. Which has led them to interpreted the wrong person. Which seems like an on going thing? That just when they think they have the killer corner. Something unexpected happens? Which leaves them to believe that Ms. Burton probably ran off? Before the police can get there to intervene with her plans. Which was just a thought? Considering that this is what she does? The fact that she want you to think one thing. When it's the total opposite of what you may think it is? Considering that they can't be to carefully about what can transpire between now & the end of the maze. That they must treat this occasion like any other catastrophe. That just because they didn't find Ms. Burton, doesn't means she is not around? That somewhere's she is waiting for the opportunity to present itself? That now, they would have to be extremely carefully about how not to get sucker by the illusions of deception?

At that point? Jason begins to look through his phone to see if there was something the killer might have left? Which would help them get a better understanding about who they are dealing with? As it turns out? That they had nothing that would show any evidence related to the crimes? However, the scariest part of it all, is not knowing what is going on? Which plays a major role on a person psyche. The fact that the killer hasn't call or left a text message. Seems pretty out of the ordinary considering how the killer loves to play mindgames. Which made them wonder that this could be one of those times. Where the killer does nothing? Which makes a person wonder what is she up too? Which is the real concern of not knowing how close she is or if she is really watching them. Which is the kind of thing that mess with a person's mind. Normally, the killer would give them the heads up about what is about to go down. Only now, the killer is reluctant to stay quiet? Leaving them to figure out what is going on? Which makes matters worse on their part of not being able to know when something bad is going to occur. Which is the solution behind this whole concept that makes for great entertainment. By having the idea of getting a person's blood boiling with adrenaline. Which makes the purpose of the chamber that much sweeter. The fact that they have to deal with all sort of distraction in the area. Which may seem as a surprise to them? On what they will encounter the far they go into the chamber. That they can expect something different each time. However, they didn't give up on finding the three faces of death masks. That there is still a chance that Ms. Burton could be hiding behind one of them. Which seems like their only option as of now? Considering how their plans always seems to fail. Which makes them wonder about a lot of things concerning this case. That has the three of them shaking their heads about the things they have to put up with.

CHAPTER 21

The Missing Link

Although, they knew the time would come when they will have to face their fears. Especially Jason for that matter? Considering that he must come to terms with his past. That the time is drawing near of determing how this thing would play out. Of what the outcome would be once the curtain goes up on the ending results. Clearly it was made to them that things aren't always what they pretend to be? That just because something is portray in a certain way. Doesn't necessary means that's what it is? Which is the first thing they must address, that being the elephant in the room. The fact that everyone wearing a scary costume poses a threat to them. Which is something they must beware at all cost? No telling who is the killer? Which also includes the staff who's job is to scare people. Although, it would seem almost impossible to try & avoid them. Do to the circumstances that they are hidden in secret confinements throughout the maze. However, their plan of seeking out one of the three faces of death masks for the killer. Seems a bit useless as time drags on? As that theory slowly starts to fade away the more things begin to evolve. Which had them thinking about other stuff. That can potentially put them in dangerous situations. Which is the many concerns they have to deal with? Considering that they are now at a crossroads of not knowing what's on the killer's agenda. That they are clueless to say the least? However, that would soon change once Jill recevie a text message from an anonymous individual. Who would explain? What will be the turning point in this case of mistaken identity? Which would shed some light on this mystery game called" The Missing Link"? That would tell the story about the issues concerning the killer Ms. Burton? Which led Jill to uncover the truth about what is going on?

What Jill had found out in the message she receive a moment ago. Seem like some sort of hint about who else maybe involve in the murders. That whoever this person was that sent her this message wanted them to know? That Elizabeth Burton has a son by the name of Danny Burton along with some other name. Which didn't say how this person is related too her. Which read the name Edgerrin James. Who's nickname is The Sandman? Jill seem delighted by this information given to her by who she believe was Lisa. Which seems fitting that it was Lisa who sent her this information. Which is to give them the heads up about who all is involve in these conspiracy murders? That got them thinking about how they could never catch Ms. Burton? Being that their are three of them. Which is all starting to make sense considering how they were under the impression that there was only one killer. That the goal was to distract the three of them from detecting what was really going on? That while they were busy tracking down Ms. Burton. Her son Danny along with someone else name Edgerrin James was the diversion. As the two of them were part of the plot to her plan. Which is to catch them when they least expect it? By surprising them with a sneak attack from all three of them. Which sums up the situation involving the incident they had with that young man. Who was wearing the michael myers costume, not long ago? The fact that it suddenly darn on them that the youngsters wearing the michael myers costume. Is indeed, Danny Burton? Which would explain why he had Jason's cellphone in his possession at the time. Claiming that he found it? Which was his only explanation at the time to cover his tracks. Considering that he wasn't expecting them to show up the way they did? That Jason's plan came through for them after all? With the help of technology by using Jill's phone to track down his phone. Which was in the hands of Danny Burton the young man in the michael myers costume.

Which is why he seem so surprise when they grab a hold to him. Not realizing that he is the son of Ms. Burton who they let slip through their fingers. That they should of known something was wrong by the way he was acting. He even indicated to them about what is going on? Once he discover that they weren't on to him. The fact that he was playing a game with a couple of friends. Which is the thing that should of tip them off? That something was wrong with this picture. It became clear to them that the people he was refering too? As friends he was playing games with? Was none other than the three of them? The fact that they had the killer in their possession & then let him go? Seem pretty discouraging? That for once? They were on the right track, but somehow they let deception over cloud their judgement. That they miss the whole object of the game which is finding the missing link? That the idea of the game is to up their IQ concerning the issues surrounding this mystery. That the clues was for them to determine fact from fiction. Which was to help them piece together the missing links to the puzzle. Which is what the killers wanted? In order for them to understand the puzzle before they die. Which is what the killers did with Lisa the first time around. Even though, Lisa survive her near death experience run in with the killer. However, there are some good & bad things that came from all of this? The good thing is that they know who Danny Burton is? The bad thing is that he may have change his appearance. Not to mention that there are still two more suspects. Who's identity is unknown at this point? Who goes by the names of Ms. Burton & Edgerrin James? Which is a real problem for the three of them. That now, they will have to face the wrath of her family as well? Which isn't good news considering that they have to get pass three psychopath's. In order to make it on the outside. Which isn't going to be an easy task?

However, there is one good thing that they have in their possession. Is the element of surprise, considering that they now know there are three killers. Something Ms. Burton doesn't realize the three of them know? That they can use this as a advantage now that they know what is going on? The fact that they know something Ms. Burton & her family don't? Which is the thing that is going to give them the edge. When the Burton family do decide's to attack them. Which is something the three of them will be prepare for? Considering that it is inevitable to happen? That this is where the line is drawn between the six of them. Based on the fact that this is where it all ends, as the final scene comes to a close. The only question that comes to mind is who will be left standing after the smoke clears. As Jill & her two buddies made it clear? That they won't give up without a fight. Which says a lot about a person's mentality when their backs are up against the wall. That a scary person is the most dangerous person to be around. At the most critical moment's when they are back into a corner. Which is where Jill & her two friends stand at this point? Even though, they must be carefully not to direct that anger toward any innocent civilian. Who soul purpose is to enjoy the show. That they must be considerate to the crowd of people in attendance. The fact that the killers are using them as a decoy. In order to create an opening to do what they need to do? Which seems very troubling to the three of them. Considering that they can't tell the diffferents on who is the killer & who's not? Especially, when it comes to being trap inside of a haunted maze. Where the object of the game is to scare a person senseless. When they are being haunted by all sort of ghouls & masked murderers. Which is something they can expect to occur inside of a haunted house? However, it seems as if the best has yet to come. As the three of them are in for a big surprise waiting on the far end of the chamber.

It seems as if they enter through another dimension in the second stage of the chamber. Where the atmosphere gets much darker? As they found themselves surrounded by all sorts of chains hanging from the ceiling. Filled with a thick fog of some sort? Which makes it harder for them to see what is around them. That all they could hear was the clicking of the chains, as they move along the room. However, once they reach a certain point in the room. They begin to hear footsteps coming from somewhere's in the room. Even though, they couldn't tell what direction it was coming from. Considering that it sounded as if it was coming from everywhere's? Although, nothing would prepare them for what happens next? That if the footsteps wasn't bad enough. Then just think of how the three of them responded when they heard someone slowly draging a chain across the floor. Which really got their blood boiling with fear? The fact that they couldn't see who it was nor where this person is? Do to the thick fog in the room that has blinded them from seeing the truth about what is going on? Then from out of nowhere's? Came this bolt of lightning that struck what looks like to be a urn? Which was something they caught from the corner of their eyes. Which created a huge spark from the electrical current? Follow by a sinister laughter that seem wicked in a way. That made the three of them feel very uncomfortable about this place. The fact that the sound alone was too terrifying to describe how it effect them emotionally. The only thing they can do at this point is to try & stay close together. Seems as though, they were in uncharted territory of not being able to see what is going on around them? Which plays a major factor on their psyche. They then begin to pick up their pace to get as far away from whoever, that is draging those chains. In doing so, they manage to stumble upon a large crystal ball? Which started to flash off & on, which made the three of them look deep into the ball.

It then started to make this beeping sound the whole while it was blanking off & on? Which had the three of them curious about what the crystal ball is going to show? It was clear that the ball has shown them a picture of someone standing behind them. Holding a couple of chains with a hideous scary costume on? Which immediately cause them to turn around only to find that there was no one behind them. According to the crystal ball that has shown them something different? Which seem as a prediction from the crystal ball? Which gives them a little idea about the person carrying around those chains. Although, they knew that they couldn't rely on what was shown on the crystal ball. Considering how the killers love to play games with them. By having them believe something that is misinterpreted to the perception. That they need to be aware of everything that go's on in this room. Then just like that? They begin to hear that same old process again? Of Having to relive those treacherous moments when the sound of chains are being drag across the floor. By someone who is constantly headed in their direction? The fact that it seem almost impossible to escape from this person. That some way or another this person seems to be on their heels where ever they go? Which is starting to get too them? Considering that they have no idea who this person is, that is following them? It wasn't long before than when they would reach a point in the room. Where they would have a moment of deja'vu with a couple of mirrors. When they would have flashes of the wrong perception. As of what is being portray in the mirrors. Like seeing their reflection in the mirror one minute? Then the next? Having someone in a scary costume charge at them with some sort of knife. Which was shown in the mirror. However, when they turn around to react to the situation? There was no one there? Which leaves them to believe that the mirrors are full of deception? Which is another way for the killers to use this as a stepping stone.

To create a distraction by using the mirrors as a certify resource as part of their plan? As part of the killers strategy to catch the three of them when they least expect it? Which creates a real problem for the three of them. Considering that the mirrors are reflecting images that is misleading. Which separates reality from fiction? Being that the killers can take full advantage of this situation. By using the mirrors special effects to impersonate one of the images in the reflection. Which makes it harder for Jill, Christian & Jason? To determine which of the killers in the mirrors image is make believe? Which is something they must figure out themselves. That just when they think that the images in the mirror is a display. It turns out to be the real deal? That instead of a projection hologram image? It turns out to be the real killer, instead? Which is something they must watch out for? Especially, when their is someone following them around the room. Who is draging chains across the floor like some sort of demented killer on the loose. Which is the thing that is so scary about this whole situation. The fact that they can never tell the differents between what's real & what's not? Not to mention? All of the scary sounds that is taking place. While all of this is happening? Although, it seems much scarier with the *rattling of the chains. That they were surrounded by? With the addition of the heavy fog that kept them from seeing what is going on around them? Which seems treacherous enough? Compare to all of the stuff they have to deal with. Which puts them at a disadvantage by all of the distractions they had to deal with all at once? However, they would receive the full effect behind this room definition of torture? When the three of them would experience fear like never before? When they encounter some of the most terrifying things imaginable. That would have them mortify about what they have experience so far?*

That had their hearts pounding with adrenaline from having so many close calls with death? To the point? Where it all felt unusually weird to them. That psychologically they were brainwash by the mirrors misfortune. That had them contemplating certain images in the mirrors reflection. Which seems torturing enough that they had to go through that? Somehow, they manage to make it pass that stage of the room without any hassle from the killers? Who is surely waiting patiently for the right moment to strike. Which will be at a time when they won't see it coming? Considering that the three of them will be so focus on trying to detect the killer amongst the crowd? That they won't notices the little things that can have such a huge impact on their lives. Like how well they can follow the signs. Which will determine the outcome on how this thing will end? That history has shown in the past that things doesn't always turn out the way it was perceived? Dating back to the time when everyone thought that Eric Johnson was the killer. That led some to believe that Jason was Eric's accomplice in these conspiracy murders. That resulted in a conflict at the end that took place that night in the galleria hall. When there were speculation that Jasmine & Thomas was the killers. Which is where things got real interesting? When they discover that Jill's two new buddies Amanda & Deshawn. Had some sort of history with Jasmine & Thomas at one point. Who at that time was consider the killers. Which brings up the situation involving Louis & Eric who they identify as being the two suspects in the halloween murders case. Which seem sort of questionable when the word got out that Raymond Spencer & Mr. Shen was the killers. Up until, Jason got caught red handed with evidence that showed he was the one responsible for the murder. That later got resolve when it was confirm that he was not the killer, according to Lisa's story? That now they are made to believe that Ms. Burton is the killer along with her son & another person who nickname is sandman.

CHAPTER 22

The Final Stage

Which is the thing that concerns the three of them about having second thought's? On how things would play out in the end as supposed to past reference where they misinterpreted the wrong impression about people who they believe was the killers? That some way or another there is always some sort of angle of conspiracy after each halloween massacre? That have to deal with some sort of speculation about how things are perceived? That maybe is interpreted the wrong way by the reality of determining fact from fiction? However, deep down they knew that the story surrounding this mystery with Ms. Burton? Stands out in every way? As being the only explanation that would sum up the cause behind these murders. According to Lisa & Jason's theory about what is going on? Seems as though, this is what it is all about? Setting the stage of seeking vengeance against those who deserve to be punishment for what they did? That trying to overlook the issue. Like it never happened, made the situation more self inflicting than they ever anticipated? That added more fuel to the fire when they try to cover it up? Which is now the consequences they have to face. All because of Eric & Jason's stupidity? Which is the least of their problems. As they must figure out how to escape the haunted maze, while at the same time stayed alive? That at this point? It seem obvious that they were going to run into the killers at some point in time? Which is the thing that concerns them the most? Considering that they can never tell when the killers are going to strike? With all of the activity that is going on around them. That the only thing they can do at this point? Is to try & prepare themselves for what's to come. As they head for the final stage of the torture chamber. It was no easy task for them as they approach the final stage. Considering that they had some run in's with close encounters during that final stretch of the second stage.

However, their situation would turn bad to worse once they enter the third dimension. Where the density of this section is much darker than the previous two? That when they enter through the gates? Fear automatically took over, as they were overwhelmed by how it was structure. It was sort of build like a underground tunnel. That had all sorts of different passages leading in opposite directions. That the only lighting in the tunnels were torches that was hanging on each side of the walls. Which didn't help the situation, considering that it was still dark inside of the tunnel. As they walk through the passage way. They would hear all sorts of weird sounds coming from other areas in the tunnel. That by coincidence? One of those sounds happen to be screams from a crying baby. That seems to be getting closer to them by the minute. Although, it was difficult for them to determine where was the screaming coming from. Do to the many passages inside of this tunnel that leds to god knows where? It seems as if the screaming child's voice begins to get louder the closer it gets to them. Which causes the three of them to panic? Considering that they have no idea about what is going on? With the sounds of what seems to be a crying baby headed their way. Considering that they well know that things aren't always what they seem to be? That they know full well that is no real baby crying? Although, they had to ask themselves the question? Was the sound following them or was they headed in the direction of the sound? Which seems like the only two explanation at this point? Considering the fact that they don't know whether they are coming or going? That their are all sorts of directions to these passages way. That by coincidence? They so happens to be headed in the direction where the sounds of the screaming baby is coming from? Which seems awfully weird? At this point? The three of them were confuse about the situation. Involving the screaming sounds of a child that seems to be getting closer to them by each passing minute.

It has gotten so bad that the child's screams begin to get much worse the closer it got to the three of them. It was so terrifying that the three of them took off like a bat out of hell? However, as they attempt to get away? They could hear the horrifying screams of a woman's voice in the background as they ran away? They then was stop in their tracks when they heard someone laughing mischievously? From one of the passage way somewhere's in the tunnel nearby? Which made them reconsider about taking certain paths. Not *knowing what they may run into? Although, it didn't matter what direction they take considering that they are now in the trenches of the maze. That this particular part of the chamber is design to bring forward the pinnacle of terror. To captive audience with absolute fear? Which is one of the many stages of the torture chamber by executing fear. Amongst those who loves to be terrify by the things that go bump in the night. Which is the thing that is so terrifying to Jill & her two friends. As they slowly made their way through the tunnel. Afraid that something will emerge from the darkness. Which is the thing they fear the most of having something unexpected happened? Considering all that is going on at the moment? As the sounds of terror echo through the passage ways of the tunnel. Which seems to be the problem with how they approach certain areas in the tunnel. Then from out of nowhere's comes this flash of light. That seems to be coming from some sort of lantern. Which is followed by some sort of weird chattering from a male's voice. That came from one of the tunnel's passage way behind them. Although, it was hard for them to see who it was? Considering that it all happen so fast. Then one by one they begin to hear the chats coming from all over the tunnel. That had them looking in every direction to see where was the voices coming from? As they seen flashes of light coming from lanterns in the distance. Which was the only thing they seen?*

However, things had begun to take form when it became apparent. That there were people who was dress in a monk robe that was carrying around lanterns. Who seem to be chatting some sort of ritual. It seems as if these people were everywhere's? The fact that it felt sort of awkward to the three of them. Being that it is sort of similar to the faces of death ritual? This however made the three of them nervous about how difficult it must be to determine the reality of this conception. That they would be fools to not think that there is more to this performance than just a show? That where ever there is conflict, lies the killer? Which is something they can be certain of? That this is where the killers loves to play mindgames. By excelling at adapting to the environment? Which means that the killers are probably impersonating one of these people who are dress in a monk robe. Which is something they must beware of, no telling what may occur? The situation would grow even worse when they begin to hear whispers in the distance. Of voices calling out to them. Whispering all sort of stuff to frightened them. It had got to the point where the voices begun to get louder the further they went into the tunnel. Although, it was hard for them to tell which direction the voices was coming from? Considering that there are so many passages in the tunnel that leads in opposite directions. Which makes it hard on them to pin point a certain spot? Based on the fact that the tunnel is dark with hardly no light to see what's ahead. Which creates a big problem for the three of them. However, they begin to speculate that the voices are coming from the people who are wearing the monk robes? Even though, the situation would get much worse when they begin to hear the sounds of terror throughout the tunnel. That in a bizzare twist? They would begin to hear the sounds of people being torture in the distance. As they heard some of the most gruesome screams they would ever hear.

Things would then get interesting when they heard someone running toward them screaming. Which cause the three of them to run as well? Considering that they are just as scare as that individual who is running toward them screaming like something is wrong. Which was their instant reaction of responding to someone else's fear. The three of them were scare out of their wits. As fear surge throughout their body as they took off running. The three of them were so much in a rush to get away? That they almost knock each other over trying to escape the madness. At that point? Things had become intense? As Christain trip & fell over Jason's foot by not paying attention to where he was going? Considering that he kept looking back to see who it was running behind them. That resulted to him falling to the floor. Christian then begin to yell out to Jason & Jill to help him? Because of the person who is still running toward them screaming uncontrolably. Like someone is after them. Which cause the two of them to stop & help Christian. Who was backpedaling with his hands while on the floor. As he try to recover by getting to his feet once more before this outrageous person reaches him. Somehow, Christian manage to get back up, but it seems as if this person was closing in on the three of them. Which cause them to get separated with Jill & Jason going one way. While Christian went another. Considering that they had no other choice being that whoever it was headed in their direction. Manage to show up at the last minute. Which cause the three of them to break up? Being that they didn't want to stand around waiting to see who this person was? That has ran up on them screaming bloodly murder? Fortunate for them, the person went in the opposite direction from them. Which was soothing to them? Although they were separated.

Which wasn't good news to for the three of them to accept the fact that they lost base with one another. Especially, doing a time like this? While, Jill & Jason are still together, but manage to lost Christian in the process. As he is left to face the treacherous of the tunnel all alone. Jason & Jill try going back for *him to see if they can find him. By calling out to him throughout the tunnel. Which is a good thing considering how the sound of their voice travels through the tunnel. Echoing throughout the passage ways of the tunnel? However, they would then receive a responds back. Which wasn't all that pleasant? Which sounded like Christian calling for help? They both begin calling out for Christian to see if it's really him. Even though, they were convince that it was him? Both of them begin to follow the sounds of Christain's voice? Which isn't a good idea? Considering that this could be a trap set by the killers to lure them into a situation. However, if it is Christian then they would be able to rescue him from god knows what? That just like the situation with Jason? The two of them wasn't going to abandon their friend. The fact that they are in this together no matter what the situation is? That although, Jason may have screw up. He was determine to make things right again by facing up to what he has done? That it takes a man to admit his mistake? That he is willing to do whatever it takes to defuse the situation by any means? That although he takes the blame for trying to cover it up? By protecting his friends from getting in trouble. After all, it wasn't him who was driving that night when the incident occur? Although, he understood repercussions that go's along with the actions he took that night. A lesson learn that somethings just never stay bury? That soon or later the truth will surface. Something he vow to not let happened again for as long as he shall live. Depending on how things turn out tonight? Which would be the turning point on how this incident reflects who he is?*

In the meanwhile, the search continue to find Christian who seems to be in some sort of danger. According to the voice that sort of resembles Christian's? They search every corner of the tunnel where they heard Christian's voice. Until, they reach the point where they discover tracks of blood on the gound. That seems to be leading some place in the tunnel. The two of them didn't know whether the blood was real or not? So they decided to follow the tracks to see where it would lead too? Hoping that the blood isn't coming from Christian. As a bit of concern grew on their faces. However, the time will come when they discover the truth about what the tunnels really represents. That for now? Jason & Jill begin to worry about Christian as they witness blood prints on the walls. Almost as if someone was putting up a struggle against an aggressor. Who seems to be draging around a wounded person. Which got them thinking about Christian? As they desperately try calling out to him to see if he was alright. Even though, there was no responds back? Which got them all upset to the point where Jill started to cry. However, just as things begin to look grim. In comes a call from Christian's cellphone. At first, Jill seem skeptical about the call figuring that maybe it's the killer. That had her contemplating whether she should answer the call. Afraid that she may receive some bad news about Christian's fate. Jason told her to be strong & that he is here with her. As he suggested the idea that she put the the phone on speaker. So that, they both can hear what is going on? As it turns out? That things wasn't as bad as they though it would be? Come to find out that Christian is alive & well. Which was a load lifted off their shoulders when they heard his voice. Which lead the two of them to ask him? Was he in any danger?

Typically, it seem very obvious to point out considering the position he is in? Which made him wonder why would they ask him a question like that? Which had Jill & Jason concern about who they was chasing around. If it wasn't Christian's voice they heard calling for help? Which had them asking where was he, at the present moment? That if he heard them calling his name a while ago? Which had Christian wondering what in the world was they talking about? It seems as if Christian didn't have a clue about what was going on? Which made it obvious that the voice they assume was Christian? Turn out to be someone else's? Which wasn't the only news they discovered? As it turns out? That this place is none other than one gigantic tombstone build for the undead? According to Christian who made the discovery that the writing is on the walls? Which got Jason & Jill to look very closely that the wall. Only to discover the Egypt symbols that is carved into the walls. By looking at the symbols on the wall it became apparent. That these symbols look mightly familiar? Which had them thinking about where they have seen this before? Then it suddenly it dawn on Jill that these are the symbols from the faces of death masks. Which was a big discovery on Jill's part? That the marking tells the story about where the three masks was originated? That although history shows that this is where the masks was originally founded during the the dark ages of time. The symbols shows where the masks came from? Which dates further back during the ancient times of Egypt? Which is something Christian has study during his time in college? It appears that the marking on the masks symbolize a greater cause for death? Considering the symbols that are carve in three masks was use as scriptures for the many types of death carry out. Toward those who are to be punish by the avenger who has the option to choose a person's death. The way he or she see's fit according to the symbols. That is now engraved into the faces of death masks?

CHAPTER 23

The Mysterious Curse

Which was design to carry the label of the Egypt symbols to spread the message to those who are marked? That the three masks was the symbol for the gypsy curse. That the avengers use to curse their enemies by marking them for death? Which resulted in some mysterious ritual killings. Which was inconspicuous concerning to the death itself? That redefine the name" Tales of the mysterious curse"? Considering all of the urban legend tales that was told about these three individual masks. Based on the formality of what the three masks stands for? That the symbols on the three masks comply with the temple of Egypt? Which is the impression Christian got from the symbols he had read on the walls? Which gives them a better understanding about the three faces of death masks. Which is why Ms. Burton decided to use them. Of what better way to exact vengeance then by using the faces of death method? Now that they understand the deal with the faces of death masks. All that is left is to unmasked the killers behind these murders. All seem well? Until, Jill & Jason seen someone shadow go by them. Thinking that maybe it's someone from the crowd who is venturing through the tunnel as well. Jason's first reaction is to see who it was that went pass them? As they both try to reach that person by calling out to whoever is in there with them. Strangely, their voices seems to travel back by the echo in the hollow tunnels. Follow by a loud banging noise that echo through the passage ways. It was then when they decided to end their conversation with Christian. In order to focus their attention on what's going on around them? That they must not lose site of what's important? Considering that they are still trap inside of the haunted maze. With three killers who is hunting them?

Afraid that the shadow they seen was probably one of the killers? Who seems to be eavesdropping on their conversation?

Considering that they had the phone on speaker the whole time they were talking? They then begin to hear rattling noises coming from nearby? Where they saw the shadow figure bypass them? Jason then told Jill to stay put, while he go & investigates what is going on? Jill refuse to let Jason go alone, while she stay behind doing nothing? That she is going to stick with him no matter what happens? Just in case something fishy occurs? Jason decided to let her come along only if she is quiet? That the plan is to sneak up on whoever is hiding amongst them. Jill however, had second thoughts about the whole thing. Afraid that they are not going to like what they find. Jill then grab Jason's hand out of fear. As they both ease closer to where they heard the noise coming from? Just as they got into position to see who it was hiding in the shadows. Jill had turn around to discover someone behind them wearing one of the monk robes holding up a knife. Who is in position to strike her down with the knife. Unfortunate for her? She begins to scream in time for Jason to pull her away. Which cause a conflict between Jason & the killer who seems pretty bent on killing him. Just as things seem at there worse? It wasn't as bad as they thought it was? As it turns out? That the person under the monk robe was an actor who was doing his job? Which was a bit of a close call for them both? Jill came up with a solution that would help them get out of the maze. She had told the man in the monk robe that she is very ill & needed some medical assistance. Jason saw the tactics she was using & decided to play along. That way the man would assist them to the exit? Where they can get help from the the police. In the meanwhile, Jason send Christian a text message explaining what they are doing. That they are going to send someone for him shortly? That it would be in his best interest to stay put until, someone comes for him.

Which they alerted the man in the monk robe that their friend is missing as well? They simply told him that they lost site of him a few minutes ago? They told the man that their friend name is Christian & that they can't leave without him. The man then reported the call to the other actors who are working in this part of the chamber. About the situation involving their friend that he related through the walkie talkie. He then told the two of them not to worry because they are going to find their friend in the matter of minutes. It would seem pointless to tell him the truth about what's going on? Considering how ridiculous it would sound being in the environment they are in? In the meanwhile, Christian found himself trap inside of a tomb with no where's to go? That if he wants to get out of this place alive. He would have to stick with the plan? To stay put, until someone shows up for him. Which seems like there is a bit of risk involve. That instead of waiting around for someone to show up? Which could be hours on hand, until they find him. He could try & locate a couple of people he can surround himself with. In hopes that it will lead him to someone who can help him out of the maze. It wasn't that long before Christian would spot somebody wearing the monk robe. Which he consider as being one of the actors who is performing one of their roles. By acting suspiciously weird to say the least. Christian then notices that the person in the monk robe. Motion his or her hand as if saying follow them. Which instantly got Christian thinking that they came through for him after all? That they finally send someone to find him? Christian being chatting with this person about what is going on? Although, he was surprise that this person actual took what he was saying seriously? As he trail behind the person in the monk robe. Do to the fact that he wanted to stay alert to his surrounding. Considering that the killer could be nearby watching them. Which sort of had him paranoid about what can he expect to happened. That there was no way the killers was going to let him escape just like that?

Christian is almost certain that Ms. Burton is going to make an attempt to catch him. Before he can even make it out of the maze. Which is something he must watch out for, considering that she can strike at any moment? Which got him all edgy about the predicament he is in? Considering that he must pay full attention to his surrounding. That he must keep his eyes open for anything unusual? Which is sort of hard to do when there are scary things going on all around you? It seems as if the actor in the monk robe. Had pointed Christian in the direction of a secret conpartment in the tunnel. Where there was a hidden slide door that leads to another section in the chamber. The person in the monk robe insisted that Christian go in first? Considering that it was their job to be courteous to the people. Christian thought that maybe this was a short cut to the outside. Only to discover that this is where the killers held Mr. Shen & Raymond Spencer hostage. Who was by the way knock unconscious tie to a pole? From that moment? Christian knew that the person in the monk robe brought him here for a reason. That reason being is to verify what's going on? Christian try attending to them, while yelling for the person in the monk robe to report this on the walkie talkie. Christian was so busy trying to assist

Raymond Spencer & Mr. Shen. That he didn't notices that the person in the monk robe was the killer. Who knock him unconscious with a piece of hard metal. That was pulled from underneath the robe. It's amazing how Christian became victimize by the illusion of a deceitful image. That all the while he was looking around for the killer? He wasn't paying no attention to what was in front of him. Being that the killer had been right beside him this whole time?

That not once? Did Christian consider the person who agree's with him that something is going on? Would hold out to be the killer? That because of the walkie talkie the killer knew what they were planning. When the call came in that two people are looking for their friend name Christian. That whoever finds him needs to bring him to the medical facility immediately? Which gives the killers the impression that they are trying to escape. Which didn't set well with the killers who made it their duty to keep them from escaping. Meanwhile, things seems to be looking up for Jill & Jason who are on their way out of the maze. Even though, there was that thought that trying to escape the maze isn't going to be easy. Considering that the killers are on standby? That although, they manage to talk their way out of the maze. With someone who knows the place like the back of their hands. Still doesn't mean that they are out of the woods yet? Considering that there is always that chance of something bizarre happening. Which seems to be one of their main concerns as of now? Which reminded Jill that she needs to check in with Christian to see how he is holding up? Not knowing that Christian is in the hands of the killers. You couldn't imagine her surprise when she receive back a text message stating that he was with someone. Who is bring him too them right now? The message also stated that they should remain where they are? Until, he is able to reach them by using the tracker the three of them share on their phones. So that, they can locate one another if need be? Just in case, one of them gets lost? Jill & Jason went along with the plan for them to stay put, until he arrives. However, they didn't have a clue that it was the killer who is sending those messages from Christian's phone.

However, it seems as if the killer had a change of heart. As the killer would send another text message to Jill's phone. Telling her that there has been a change in plans. That instead of waiting around for him to show up? He thought that it would be a better idea if they meet him at a certain spot in the tomb? Jill would then ask the man in the monk robe could he take them to the area where the signal is on her phone. Which is where her friend Christian is waiting for them. The man agree to take them to the area where they are to meet up? Not realize that they are falling right into the killers trap. Who is using Christian's phone as a way to lure them straight into the killers hands. Which is something they are unaware of? Although, they were still under the impression that the killer is somewhere's around hiding? When actual they are headed right in the direction of the killers who has manipulated them time & time again? That the moment of truth is drawing near? Which will determine how this thing will play out in the end? Based on what's at stake? Of them not realizing that they are being set up? That the conclusion of this game all comes down to these final minutes. As of what the outcome would be when the curtain goes up on the ending results. Of who will be left standing when it's all said & done. Which brings up the question about the conspiracy of how it all connects together? Seems as though, if it's one gigantic puzzle that is shattered into a million pieces. With the comparison to the missing links in the chain that connects together these murders. Which is something Jason & Jill are looking forward too? As of getting to the bottom of all this drama surrounding Jason & Ms. Burton. That there needs to be a point where the two of them draw the line. Whether it's by settling their differents with a game of death or coming to some sort of understanding. With leaves them to believe that this will end in violence.

That there is no getting around the fact that Ms. Burton wanted to settle the score with Jason. In order to carry out the rest of her sentence by wiping the slate clean. Considering how the rain washes everything away? Getting rid of all the bad rubbish that the storm has created. That when it's all said & done the sun would shine once again? Which is a message that was sent to Jason's phone from the killer. Who use record audio to related the message to him. Which got Jason thinking that Ms. Burton is up to something. That she is planning her escape just like she has in the past? That had the two of them thinking that Ms. Burton probably has already left the scene. Leaving behind her son & Edgerrin James aka" Sandman" to take over on her behalf? That no one would suspect them as being the killllers. Considering that she has everyone fool by thinking that she acted alone in these killings. The plan was simple? That when the police arrive on the scene. They are going to be looking for her? In which, she will be long gone by than? Which is where things get complicated? When she is nowhere's to be found. However, what Ms. Burton didn't know is that Jason & Jill found out about her son & Edgerrin James. Who are assisting her in these murders? Which gives them the upper hand. On what should they be expecting? Thanks to Lisa, who came through for them once again. When she tip them off that there was two more killers along with Ms. Burton. It wasn't long before than when they would reach the spot where they suppose to meet up with Christian. Thanks in large part to the employee for getting them there. Who knows his way around the maze even with a blindfold? However, this place they were in, was much scary than the tunnel itself. The fact that they enter into some sort of secret cave where there was no one other than them around. Which seem a bit unusual as of why they pick this spot to meet up?

CHAPTER 24

The Moment Of Truth

As a bit of suspicion over came the two of them about how fishy this thing is starting to look. When there wasn't any sign of their friend to be found. Which seems a bit strange considering that he hasn't shown up yet? Which had them thinking that something bad must of happened to them? Jill & Jason started to get concern? As they begin calling out to Christian to see if he was somewhere's around? However, when they wasn't getting any responds back from him. The two of them begin to get worry that something bad may have happened to him. Not to be discourage by the lack of fate? The two of them remain hopeful that Christian will turn up soon or later? As a sense of relief was felt when they heard someone's voice in the distance. That had the three of them thinking that it was one of the employee headed their way with Christian. As it turns out? That it was definitely someone who works here? Who had on the exact same monk robe as the rest of the employee's. Although, it was hard for them to tell who it was under the hoodie. Which had Jill & Jason kind of suspicious about who it is? Considering that whoever it is hiding in the monk robe could be an imposter? Which seems to be the case considering how this person is behaving. As this mysterious individual made a gesture with his or her hands to the three of them. By signaling them to come over to the spot where this mysterious person is standing? Which got Jill & Jason curious about wanting to know you this person is? As they demanded that the person identify themselves? Being that they didn't want to take any chance of falling for a case of mistaken identity. As time has shown before that things aren't always what they seem to be? The man who is helping them thought that they were being foolish. As he try to explain that the person in the same monk robe as him? Is a fellow co-worker who is doing their job by promising to bring their friend too them, just like they ask?

Not to be fool by what the two of them see as a potential misconception of what is happening? Which seems all too familiar to the two of them on what they should be expecting? After years of being manipulated by the system use by the killers? That now, they finally caught on to the game that is being played on them. Which is something some people would never understand? As they try to warn the man that this was no co-worker of his? However, just to keep down the confusion the man ask? The person dress in the monk robe to identify him or herself to hopefully resolve the issue. To get the two of them to relax a bit? As it turns out? That the person would indeed identify who they are? When it became apparent once the person pulled out a knife with blood on it. Which made a huge statement about who it is? However, just as the killer begin charging toward them? The man quickly made a beeline to run in the opposite direction. Pushing Jill & Jason out of his way as he turn to run. Only to insert himself onto a knife that impaled him the moment he turn around to run. By the other killer who was standing behind them with the knife. Dress in the baby slasher costume from the horror movie" Valentine"? The man was stun as he gradually back away from the knife? That was insert into his stomach? Which he started to hold the moment the killer pull it out from his stomach. The man then fell to the ground in a panic mode. As Jill try to comforter the man by telling him it's okay? Until, he gradually took his final breath before dying. It was at that moment when reality would eventually kick in? That the time has come for them to face their fears by confronting their tormentors. Which would be the icing on the cake as of how things play out? As the two killers threaten to take the final approach in the preparations for their demise. Which is the final stage in the game of chance considering that their number is up?

However, Jill & Jason had a trump card that reveals who the two killers are? That got her explaining about who they believe are the killers that is hiding behind the masks? Which caught both of the killers attention when Jill called out their names? That being Danny Burton & Edgerrin James aka" Sandman"? That they know just as well who it is? That the discovery was made when Christian recently pull off the mask. Revealing who Danny Burton is? Which prove substantially correct as Danny begins to remove the hoodie, revealing his true self? Along with Edgerrin James who started to pull off the baby killer mask from the horror movie" Valentine"? You couldn't imagine their shock?

When the truth was reveal about who the two people was behind it all? As the expression on their faces was priceless? That the person they thought was Danny? Who they suspected was the young man wearing the Michael Myers costumes. That had Jason's cellphone has turn out to be the wrong person. To their surprise the two suspects were none other than Dr. John Edwards & Officer James Dwight? Who's real names were Danny Burton & Edgerrin James. As it turns out that Officer Dwight was Danny Burton & Dr. Edwards was Edgerrin James. Which brings up the situation on how the discovery was made? It seems as if Officer Dwight was under the impression that Jill was refering to the time. When Christian accidentally pull the mask off his face which is where he thought they discover who he was? As suposed to what Jill was refering too? When Christian pull off the Michael Myers masks that the young man had on? Which happened on two separate occasion with the masks being pulled off? Which is where all of the confusion took place? Seems as though, they both wasn't on the same page? Concerning the issue with the mask being pulled off? As there seems to be some confusion between both parties? As of what just happened? That had Officer Dwight aka Danny Burton & Dr. Edwards aka Sandman? Seem just as surprise as Jill & Jason that things would turn out this way? Which is something unexpected for them all?

Which seems kind of unusual the way it all transpire that had the two killers wondering was this all coincidental? That Jill & Jason knew who they really were? That judging by their expression when it was confirm that Officer Dwight & Dr. Edwards was the killers? It seem as if the looks on their faces says it all? That they didn't have a clue about what was going on? That the two of them were shock to find out that it was them this whole time. It would then become clear to the killers that Jill & Jason didn't have the slightest clue about what is going on? Considering that Jill & Jason demanded to know the where'a'bout of one Ms. Elizabeth Burton? Which cause Danny to shake his head in disbelief? Considering how dumbfounded the two of them were? Based on how blinded they are of understanding the reality of the puzzle? That is place right in front of their eyes. That the maze sort of represents what's going on here? That the concept is to figure out the layout of this puzzle. In order to make sense of something they don't understand? That the answers has been specify throughout the maze? That all they needed to do was to follow the signs? Which would indicate that Jason is a killer? Which is something Danny & Mr. James wanted Jill & Christian to see? That all because of some *misunderstanding? Their cover got blown which wasn't part of the plan? Which led Danny to believe that someone may have tip them off? Which is how they knew about the two of them? However, they were still clueless about what is going on? So, Danny & Mr. James decided to let them in on a little secret? By setting the record straight about what is going on here?*

Considering how Jill & Christian thought that the two of them were dead after all this time. Danny Burton would go on to tell the story about how it all got started? Dating back to the night where his mother was killed? That whether Jason & his friends knew it or not? That there was someone who witness the incident with his mother being struck by Eric's car that night. That when Jason & his buddies decided to leave the scene of the crime. The person who witness it all? Told him & Mr. James what happened to her? When they arrive on the scene minutes later? Considering how they were schedule to meet up with her before the incident occur? Based on the fact that Ms. Burton had a little accident of her own. Which is why she called her son & Mr. James to come out to help her? Considering that she had no other way to get home that night. Although, she wasn't hurt in the accident, her car sustain some serious damage. As she was on her way home from the rehearsal dinner. Considering that she was schedule to get married the next day to Edgerrin James. Which is where things is starting to make sense? As of why the two of them would go on a murder spree? Which was just the beginning on how things would escalate? However, when they arrive on the scene, it became clear to the both of them. That Elizabeth Burton was pronounce dead from the injuries she sustain in the incident. When she was struck by Eric Johnson's car. For some apparent reason Danny didn't report the incident right away? Being that he was a cop & all? Instead, they decided to bury his mother deep in the woods that same night. Before the police could get there. To make it seem as if Jason & his friends try to cover up what they did, by getting rid of the body? Which was one way to get even with them for killing Mr. James fiance & Danny's mother. That this is what they get for committing a murder & than take off, like nothing happened?

Which brought some attention to the case considering that it was reported that Elizabeth Burton was missing? That the plan was to let this story run it's course. Until, it becomes national news where Jason & his friends could be portrayed as america's most wanted criminals. However, it seems as if someone interfere with their plans? That someone being Louis's father who Eric's mother hired to make this thing go away? In order to protect her son from going to jail? Which was how Eric manage to cover it up, through his mother who had the finances to make it all disappear? Which is why Danny & Mr. James decided to kill Eric's mother in a supposedly armed robbery. That by Danny being a policeman he investigated Louis's father for fraud. Which is why he was sent to the slammer. Where he was incarcerated with the very people he had screwed over? Which resulted in his untimely death? The same could be said about Louis's mother who was killed as well, a few days earlier. Which turn their attention to Eric who they set up to take the fall for the very first murders in the halloween massacre. Follow by the second one, which also involves Jason as Eric's accomplice? That if they wasn't going to take the fall for killing his mother? Then they would take the fall for killing innocent people on halloween? It seem as if their plan was going to work out perfectly that night in the galleria hall. Until, one of the ghostface masks gets pull off that ruin it all? That the object of the game was for the four of them to killed one another. Considering that they all had on the same costume from the movie" Scream"? That unfortunately, they didn't know what to expect from seeing each others reflections in the mirrors that night. Which sort of played into the whole scheme of things. That the goal was for them to kill each other & then have Eric & Jason come along. Just when the police arrive on the scene to catch them in the act? Considering that there were reports that the two of them were the ones doing all of the killings. Which didn't go as well, like they plan? In which they had to improvised by setting up Jasmine & Thomas to take the fall? Considering that their plan had fail & that the police was already on their way to the galleria hall?

Which brings up the incident with Louis & Eric the following year in the woods. When they went down to Jason's father cabin unwillingly? Where Danny & Mr. James proceeded to pick up where they left off one year ago? When they continue to torment Louis about the death of his girlfriend Ashley. Who's body was disfigure inside of a dryer? That sort of disappear when he try to show his friends what had happened? Only to find out later that the killer had place Ashley's disfigure body inside of Louis house. That was later discovered by the police who search Louis house after the police receive an anonymous tip from someone. As it turns out? That someone was the very man who set this whole thing up? That person being the Sandman" Edgerrin James? Who was the one responsible for killing Ashley & then place her body inside of Louis's house. In order to set him up? That by Danny being a cop

& all? He did what was necessary to necessitate Louis by having him think that the police has enough evidence against him. To put him away for life for killing his girlfriend? Considering that the police did find her body inside of his house. Somehow, the killer manage to get Louis to come down to Jason's father cabin. Under false pretense? To where the party was held in the woods near Jason's father cabin. It was then, when Louis got the impression that Lisa & her team was there because of him. Do to a little persuasion from the killer who instigated the situation? By telling Louis that Lisa is a undercover reporter who is secretly investigating him? That she is the informant for the police? Which means that the police is already in the area. Getting into position in order to capture him? That's when Louis kidnap Alan & force him to the news van. To gather the evidence they had on him? Wearing the exact same costume as the killer, that being the mask of pain? Which was use in many of the killings, that automatically labels him as a suspect for sure. That resulted in him taking the disc & Alan's phone so he couldn't call the police. It was only after Louis left, that the killer would show up & murder Alan? Which was none other than the Sandman, Edgerrin James. By that time, Louis was trying to make it out of the area before the police came? Only to find out that he was too late, as he heard the sirens of the police cars approaching. At that point, he panic & made his way through the cornfield. To avoid running into the police? According to what he believe's in his mind is happening? When the truth was that Lisa was there to investigate the halloween murders? That her main concern at that time was Jill, Jason & Christian who were the targets.

It was foolish of him to let the killers determine his fate? Although, he had no idea that Danny Burton was a policeman who had filled his head with all sorts of nonsense? That landed him in the graveyard? When the police took him to be the killer?That by him having on the scarecrow costume already makes him a suspect? That this was his only way to hide from the police who was susposedly after him? That ended up with him taking Lisa hostage with a sickle held to her neck? That the only way he could escape the police was in Lisa's news van. Which we all know how that situation ended? With him being killed by the people he swore was after him? Which brings up the case with Eric Johnson who try to get Jason's or Jill's attention the whole night? Hoping that one of them would catch onto what he was doing? By drawing attention to himself by acting suspicious? When that didn't work? He decided to wait for the opportunity when he can catch one of them alone? So that, he can reveal himself to them. Considering that he needed to have on a costume to stay clear from everyone? Being that the police was still looking for him? Which is why he waited, until halloween? So that, he can come up out of the shadows? Which is the one time he can walk the streets without anyone noticing him. Something the killers would be expecting him to do? That when the time comes. Eric is going to try & get in touch with the others, in order to help them, but to do that? He would need a disguise? Which was something the killers hope he would do? In order for their plan to work? That by him wanting to wait to catch one of them alone? Played a significant role in his death? By not realizing the importants of the cause & effect symptoms. Made the outcome of sealing his fate seem as if it was scripted? That there wasn't any other way this could of gone. That there would be some sort of consequences for sneaking up on a person who's life is in danger. Which happened when Eric crept up on Jill the night when she killed him?

CHAPTER 25

The Last Stand

It seem as if they all got the wrong impression about Eric that night. Seems as though, he was the accuser in the faces of death murders conspiracy? That judging from their perspective that if the shoe fits the crime? Then the picture is worth a thousand words. According to imagine that labels Eric Johnson as the killer? That just because a person has on a scary costume toting around a knife. Automatically, assume that they are the killer. Not realizing that things aren't always what they seem to be? That they should ever judge a book by it's cover? The fact that Jill's eyes had deceive her that night when she killed Eric Johnson. As it was made clear to her that the goblin mask was just a disguise. So that, no one would notices him? Second of all, he carry around the knife for his protection. Which she misunderstood? Thanks to Danny & Mr. James mindgames. That ended up with her doing the two of them a huge favor by killing Eric Johnson. Considering that there was no use in getting involve, when she could do the job for them? Which made Jill furious at the two of them? Which brings up the question about how they manage to get this far without being detected? Which is really a good question as of how they manage to do all of this without being caught? Edgerrin James begin to explain the situation to them. About how they manage to get away with it? That a portion of it all contains to Danny being a police officer. Considering that he knows how the law works? Which means that there are ways around the law? The fact that Danny can make things appear in a certain way. With the help of a scientist who studies physics of human anatomy. Creating the perfect formula for the inquiring minds? The fact that they are like two peas in a pod. Based on how they manage to stay ahead each time?

Starting with Professor Dell Fraser who they murder, in order to get to Jason? Considering that it wasn't nothing personal? It was only to replace him? Seems as though, science was Mr. James field of study? That the plan was to wait to see who would replace Professor Fraser as the class new instructor? In which they would go after Mr. Fraser replacement. Which was a guy by name of Dr. John Edwards? Who was killed by Edgerrin James before anyone knew who he was? It was then? When Edgerrin James would step in for Dr. Edwards by pretending to be him. That all the while long? Mr. James was impersonating Dr. Edwards as the first semester of school begin. Which was only temporary, until he was able to gather the information needed to give to Danny Burton about Jason & his friends. Who was there also under a false name as a temporary officer? To help patrol the streets around the city for halloween? Considering the murders that took place on the southside of the city a year before? However, when Mr. James got all of what they needed? He decided to fake his own death? By placing the real Dr. Edwards body inside of the house where he was staying at the time. Only to burn it down with him inside. That led everyone to believe that Dr. Edwards was dead? According to the dental records that confirmed it was him. Do to the fact that his body had been burn to a crisp? Not realizing that the man they believe to be Dr. Edwards was nothing more than a imposter? Who manage to pull the wool over everyone's eyes with that little stunt he pulled? Which is how Danny Burton aka Officer Dwight fell off the radar as well? That being a volunteer to assist other officers that night to patrol the streets? Was the cover he needed to get the ball rolling? That once he got everything going? He too fake his death? By having Jill & Christian think that he had been murder by the killer? When they were on there way to the galleria hall to help Jasmine.

Which brings up the situation about Ms. Elizabeth Burton role in all of this? That when their first plan didn't work in trying to get the networks to cover the story about her disappearance? In hopes that it would make Jason & Eric out to be murderers who try to get away with it? However, when that plan failed, do to some interference from Louis father? It seems as if burying her was the best thing they could of done? Considering how it all plays into the whole scheme of things? Considering that she is out to seek vengeance against them for what they have done. Which is what they wanted Lisa to believe. When they sent her those pictures in the envelope to her house telling her to follow the signs. That since she was determine to solve the mystery? They gave her a story *that is sure to make headlines? By getting Lisa to sell the story about what she just stumble upon? That Elizabeth Burton is the killer? Considering how it all traces back to her? Given the scenario of the story? According to the evidence they have provided to make it seem that way? Based on how this story was perceived? Which indicated that Elizabeth Burton attempted to kill Lisa after learning the truth behind the mystery of the halloween murders. That there is always a small price to pay when sticking your nose where it doesn't belong? That the goal is for them to go after a killer who doesn't exist? That since they bury her at a secret location? The story of Elizabeth Burton would seems more substantial? Which would be an excellent urban legend tale? Considering how no one could find her body after she got run over. By a couple of drunk teenagers out driving that night? Who all started to die mysteriously on halloween night along with their friends? Which will have many to believe that it was Elizabeth Burton who has return from the brink of death to carry out her death sentence for those who are marked.*

By using the costumes of famous slashers from the horror movies to exact her vengeance. By marking them for death with the curse of the three faces of death masks. That the best part of the story is that her disappearance remains a mystery to this day? Which is a perfect folk tale story to tell around the campfire? Which would be one out of a hundred stories mention surrounding the tales of the faces of death mythology? Considering how people are tormented by the fear of death which is the slogan for the faces of death masks. That in order for the two of them to get away with it all? Is to tie up all of the loose ends? Meaning that they need to dispose of all three of them? Including the person who decided to spill the beans by giving the three of them hints on who it was behind the murders. Which is none other than the witness who knows more about what is going on? Jill & Jason both was intrigue by Danny & Mr. James story of how it all went down? Considering how the pieces of the puzzle are finally starts to become clear? Connecting together the missing links in the chain? It appears that Danny Burton & Edgerrin James has set the tone. For putting them in tough situations that seems to spiral out of control. Each time they are put to the test by the killers who knows their weakness? Like for example? That Jason is weak minded when it comes to Jill? The fact that the killers has been using Jill to get too him? While, Eric Johnson was willing to do anything to prove he was innocent? Which was his downfall? That also claim the life of a private investigator named George Larusso who apparently bit off more than he can chew. By getting involve in something that doesn't concern him. Which intensify the story even more when there is a bit of foul play involve in his death? Which brings up Louis who was sort of paranoid. From all the threats he receive. Do to his father's actions? That played a huge role in his death? Which turns the attention to Lisa who didn't know when to quit? Which landed her in the hospital. However, time was beginning to run out for the two of them? As Danny Burton & The Sandman aka" Edgerrin James"? Begin to make the final preparations to get rid of the problem that stands before them? Which has Jill asking? What did they do with Christian? Which is a very uncommon thing to ask? Considering that Christian should be the least of their worries? That there are more important things to worry about? As Danny begin to run his finger slowly across the knife? That once they are dead there will be no one else to identify the two of them? Except for the witness who will pay the ultimate price for betraying them. As it turns out? That person was none other than Lisa? Who Jill & Jason believe notify them of the situation?

Which had the killers thinking that the authorities will have nothing to trace? Except for the fact that they are going to be chasing a ghost? That soon the truth will spread across the country about the mysteries behind the murders? Which will have many people wondering was it all premeditated? Considering the issues with the conspiracy theory that surround's this case? That will go down in history as one of the most bizarre tragedy anyone has seen? As the time begin to draw near for Jill & Jason to decide on what they should do? As of how they were going to make a stand against the two of them? Although, there was little time to think of what they can do? Considering that time was running out for the two of them to make up their minds? Which cause Jason to react in such a way? Do to the amount of pressure he was under at the moment? Considering that there was no time to think when face with a decision that will determine their lives. As Jason shoved Danny into Edgerrin James. Which gave them the little time they needed to get away? Which would give them more time to figure out what to do? Knowing that there was no way the killers are going to let them escape. Knowing what they know? Somehow, they manage to find their way back to the tunnel. Which is a good thing considering that there are people around who can help them? Although, it would be wise if they take different passage ways in the tunnel. In order to keep the killers off their heels. Which didn't do no good considering that the killers are keeping pace with them. Lucky for Jiil & Jason they manage to find a group of people who was venturing through one of the tunnels. Jill then begin to scream for the people in the group to help them? Thinking that it's part of the show the people took it as some sort of game? As they too begin to run. That from Jill & Jason expression the people didn't know what to make of it? As they also ran through the tunnel screaming & yelling? Which had the people wondering what was Jill & Jason running from?

They all ran into a dead end of the maze where Jill & Jason must back track their steps. Which means that they would have to get pass the killers. In order to head in another direction? However, when they turn around the killers was no where's to be found? In which the group of people found it to be pretty entertaining? As of how they set up the stage of having everyone think that someone was after them? When in reality? They have no clue about what is going on? As they all was curious to see what Jill & Jason has in store for them next? As the people took the two of them to be some sort of tour guide. Which is exceptional news for Jill & Jason to have some sort of security blanket. Just in case something should go wrong? That instead of telling them the truth? Jill & Jason decided to go with the flow of things. Seems as though, they can benefit from this? By staying clear of the killers if they use the crowd of people to their advantage. However, there is always that chance of something unexpected happening? Where there are all sorts of surprises at every turn. Which means that they would have to keep their eyes open for anything unusual? Although, the two of them were just as afraid as the people in the group. Even though, they couldn't tell by how good of a job Jason & Jill is doing. Selling the whole tour guide look? Then from out of nowhere's came this person dress in a scary outfit? Like some sort of maniac from a horror film who had a sickle in his hand. Bearing down on Jason's face as the two of them were in a struggle of total supremacy. While the crowd look on? As if they were amaze by what they thought was a good performance from the two actors? That if they didn't know better, they would of thought that it was real? Judging from the emotions of Jill's reaction when the attack occur? Between Jason & the killer who begin to get the upper hand. However, the results always remains the same? When it comes to these sort of things. That there is always something peculiar about the person they suspect is the killer? Of having to realize time & time again?

That things aren't always what they attend to be? As the person who attack Jason was just an actor doing his job? Which got a standing ovation from the crowd who thought that it was a marvelous performance? However, it was a close call for Jason who's life flash before his eyes? Considering all of the suspense that is spontaneous in every aspect of the equation. Which is a lot for three person to handle in one night? Seems as though, this has been going on for quite sometime now? That they had to put up with being harass by the killers mindgames? That maybe it's time for them to flip the script on the killers. By using their own technique against them? To give Danny Burton & Edgerrin James a dose of their own medicine. That in order to do that, they must come up with a plan? That would benefit them to seize the opportunity when it comes? Unfortunately, the tables would turn on Jill & Jason? As the killers begin bearing down on the two of them from behind? Even with the crowd standing around looking as if this is part of the show. Not realizing that the people hiding behind the monk robe & the scary baby costume from the slasher film" Valentine" are not actors? That had the group of people watching in suspense. As the killers slowly approach Jill & Jason who has no idea the killers is closing in on them? It wasn't until they heard Christian's voice on the walkie talkie. That one of the killer's was carrying around at the time. That they realize that the killers are behind them? Safe to say? That Christian warn them right before the killers were getting ready to strike? Which means that Christian somehow escape & was no longer knock unconscious. From the blow he had suffer at the hands of the killer? That the killers made a critical mistake when they left Christian unattended in a secret room in the tunnel? With the person who knows how the maze is structure. Considering that this person is the architect behind the design. That person being Mr. Wang Shen who was discover by Christian along with Raymond Spencer? Who was knock unconscious tie to a pole. Before he too, fell at the hands of the killer who fool him with the whole monk robe look? That had Christian thinking that the person wearing the monk robe was an employee sent to help him?

CHAPTER 26

The Conclusion

However, the thing that concerns the killers is the possibility that Christian may have escape the maze. Along with Raymond Spencer & Mr. Shen who may have alerted the authorities about what is going on? Which is a huge momentum swing as the roles were reverse. As Christian begin using reverse psychology on Danny & Mr. James. By giving them a dose of their own medicine. By using their own technique against them with quotes from the horror movies? That have to deal with a lot of scary questions? That the best part of it all? Is giving the killers an ultimatum of what fate has in store for them? As the mindgames begin to take it's affect on Danny & Mr. James. As of where is Christian hiding? Considering that he was able to warn his friends that they were in danger. Which means that he is somewhere's nearby watching things, as it unfolds? It seems as if Danny Burton & The Sandman aka Edgerrin James started to lose their cool? When Christian begin antagonizing them both with all sorts of games that is being played on them? When people from all over the tunnel wearing scary masks begin moving from one place to another. Sort of like the game of hide & seek? Where the hunters would become the hunted? Considering how the tables have turn? By making matters worse for the killers who have to seek out which scary costume is Christian hiding under? As Christian was able to quote the famous phase to the killers? Of what is their favorite scary movie of all time? Follow by the theme song from the movie Jaws that is playing on the loudspeaker? Which is a perfect violation to undergo? Considering how the song is implicating what's going on around them? Which even had the crowd of people scare of what may surface? Although, they didn't have the slightest clue about what is going on? It seem as if Danny & Edgerrin

James was so focus on Christian? That they didn't realize that Jill & Jason have manage to distance themselves from the two of them?

Which was brought to their attention when someone in the group notice that they were leaving? Which is where all of the chaos ensued? When the temple of the Jaws song begin to intensify? Which is where the people dress in scary costumes came charging every which way at the group of people standing by? Which includes Danny Burton & Edgerrin James who was unprepareed to handle the raid of people coming toward them with weapons? Which cause a disruption within the group of people. Which was Jill & Jason chance to get away from the killers. Although, Danny spotted them trying to get away & went after them? While, Edgerrin James stood in the crosshairs of being maul by the crowd. As he was being push around like some rag doll? By the people who are demonstrating what took place with the faces of death ritual? By wearing the masks along with the monk robe, which is how the killings was done during those times? Which was just suposed to be a demonstration? However, it seem as if Christian took full advantage of the opportunity by getting in a few good stabs with the knife he was carrying around? Even though, it was hard to tell which person was doing the stabbing. Based on the fact that everyone had on the same costume carrying around knives. Which wasn't suposed to real? As Danny try to make his way through the crowd? In order to get to his stepfather in time before Christian could get to him? Which seem impossible? Considering all of the pandemonium that is taking place. That the only way Danny could get to his stepfather is to pull out his gun & start shooting. Which had everyone scattering to get away? However, once Danny reach his stepfather Edgerrin James? He was a little to late to save him. As he had to watch his beloved stepfather die in his arms? In which, he became real angry over the situation & decided to take that anger out on Jill & Jason? As Danny begin shooting at the two of them?

Jill & Jason begin to run through the tunnels ducking for cover, as Danny took aim at them. Considering that now he has lost two people he loved so much? At was taken from him by the person who he blames for all of this? That is trying again to cover his tracks? With the help of his friends who apparently don't understand the principles of it all? That had Danny thinking that if he goes down? Then he is going to take them with him? Which will wipe the slate clean as the only loose end to the puzzle? Considering that their is nothing else to live for? However, Jill & Jason seem to have a different approach about life?

As they were determine to make it out of this thing alive, but fate would allow that to happened? As Jason took a bullet to the leg that ended their attempt to escape? It seem as if the game was over for the two of them. As Danny Burton took aim at Jill's head with the gun? Pressing it to her skull, as he slowly pull the trigger? Which had Jason outrage considering that there was nothing he could do to stop it? As Jill look into Jason's eyes with sorrow? Explaining how she will always love him? Which is when Danny pulled the trigger of the gun to take away Jill's life? Just as Jason took the lives of his mother & stepfather. That he too, will know what it is like to lose someone he cares about? That this will haunt him for the rest of his life, as Danny decided not to kill him. However, he is going to make Jason regret the things he has done? By taking away the one thing that he loves? However, it seems as if the gun got jammed for some reason. Which was a sign of relief for Jill as she saw her chance to get away? Before Danny Burton could unjammed the gun? In which Jason took it upon himself to knock the gun out of Danny's hands with his other foot? Which ended with Danny going after Jill as she attempts to get away? While, Jason try his hardest to go after them, but fail to do so? Considering that he was in to much pain to stand up? Which had Jason concern that Jill may not make it on the outside?

Which infuriated Jason that he is rendered helpless to protect Jill from the killer. That he would ever forgive himself if something was to happened to her. That regardless of the pain he is in? There was no question that he must protect the girl he loves? Lucky for Jason? Christian had come along to see if they were alright. Jason told Christian about the situation Jill is in? As he beg Christian to help save her from the ruthless killer who is on a rampage? Jason then suggested that Christian take the gun with him that Danny had left behind. Christian told Jason not to worry because he is going to put an end to it all? That he can bet his last dollar on it? In the meanwhile, Jill found herself scrambling for a way out of the maze. With Danny hot on her trail? Considering that it wasn't long before Danny would eventually catch up to her? As an all out brawl ensued between the both of them. As Jill did all she could to defend herself from the killer? Who begin strangling her in a violent rage, as he begin insulting her. By telling her it's all her boyfriend's fault that she is in this predicament? Seems as though, Jill was a fighter, she manage to break free of the chokehold. By kicking him in the groin? Which only made the fight between the two of them more violent? That even though, Jill put up a good fight? She was no match for Danny who manage to get the upper hand. Which led to him pinning her against the wall, in order to pull the knife out. From underneath the monk robe to finish her off? It seem as if Christian got there just in the nick of time before Danny could do any harm to Jill? At that point? Christian warn Danny to let her go? Instead of letting her go, Danny use Jill as a shield by placing her in front of him. While, holding the knife to her throat? As he too, begin making threats by making it plain & simple. That Jill's life hangs in the balance considering that it is up to him to determine whether she lives or dies? That the choice is totally up to him? Christian knew what was at stake when he didn't back down.

Considering that Danny is going to kill her anyway, even if he puts down the gun. Which is a sure thing for Danny to make an attempt at him. Once the gun is no longer in the equation that can be use against him? Considering how desperate Danny is? Now that he has nothing to lose, which makes him a very dangerous person to be around? Not knowing what he attends to do? Considering his condition at this time of someone who is unstable? Which means that Christian mustn't do anything that would jeopardize his friend's life? That he must be careful of the things he do or say? Considering that he doesn't want to set off the bomb that is ticking away in Danny's brain. However, he wasn't going to let go of the gun under no circumstances? Being that it's his only line of protection to keep Danny from killing Jill? Although, time is beginning to run out for them all? Seems as though, the police will be there shortly? Considerng that he sent Mr. Shen & Raymond Spencer to alert the authorities about what is going on? That if he goes? He could take Jill with him. Which is why he must come up with a solution to save Jill before the police get there? Which is something Jill realize as well? Considering that she needs to come up with a plan & quick? In which she came up with a perfect plan to get Danny's attention. By getting him all work up over the death's of his family? As Jill begin trashing Danny's mother & stepfather with all sorts of nasty remarks? Which doesn't seem like the smart thing to do? As Christian was wondering what in the world is she doing? That saying bad stuff about Danny's mother & stepfather isn't going to make things better for her. That the only thing it is going to do? Is get her killed? Which is exactly is going to happened if she doesn't stop her foolishness? Judging by how angry Danny is starting to get? That all she is doing is setting herself up to be killed? Which is something Christian couldn't bring himself to understand?

Jill kept on with the insults, until it became irritating for Danny who just lost it? Which was the opportunity Jill was waiting for? As she waited for Danny to get all belligerent to the point where he drops his guard? Which is where Jill manage to escape from his grip by biting his hand the one with the knife in it? Which gave Christian a clear shot at Danny chest. Once Jill move out of the way? Which was the clearance Christian needed to take the shot? However, it seems as if the gun was still jammed? Which put Christian in a bad spot, as Danny came charging at him with the knife? At that point? Christian try pulling the trigger multiple of times. Until, the gun finally was able to fire off a few rounds that was left in the clip? Which ended in suspense? Considering how close Danny was to him? That the gun finally gave way to put the breaks on Danny's momentum? Which was crazy of how intense that moment was for him? The bullets did the job, as Danny drop to the floor almost instantly after being shot multiple of times in the chest? It seems as if a load has been lifted off their shoulders. When it was clear that Danny Burton is dead? Jill then ran over to Christian & gave him a big huge. Thanking him for coming after her? Which is a big deal considering what they been through? It was then when the police started to arrive on the scene? Which had Jill & Christian shaking their head? Do to the fact that they always arrive when everything is over? They then went to see about Jason who is probably stress out? Of not knowing the verdict of what remains of his two friends? Which was put aside when he saw the two of them together in one piece. Which made him smile knowing that they are okay? As the paramedic came to the rescue to work on his injure leg. It seems as if Jason was grateful to have friends such as Jill & Christian. Who stood by him through it all? Which is what friendship is all about? As Jill gave Jason a kiss on the cheek to remind him of the love she still feels for him?

As Jill made it clear to the paramedics that they don't leave without her. Considering that she wanted to ride alongside her boyfriend in the ambulance? That Christian is going to meet up with her there at the hostipal? They both told Jason to be strong as the paramedics carry him away on the stretcher? It seems as if Jill & Christian finally found their way out of the haunted maze? Considering that they were already at the end? That the third stage of the torture chamber was the final attraction in the maze. However, once they reach the outside it seem as if a terrorist attack the theme park? As there were cops everywhere's? Filled with news reporters from different locations to cover this story? They would soon meet up with Lisa who manage to find her way there? That it was her job to uncover the truth about these murders? In which she succeeded in doing as a job well done? According to Jill & Christian who couldn't of done it without her. That she is the reason why they discover who Edgerrin James & Danny Burton was? Which kind of had Lisa confuse about what they were refering too? Which sort of made Jill & Christian a bit baffle of who sent them the text message letting them know about Danny & Edgerrin James? If it wasn't Lisa, who they believe was the one who had sent it to them? That according to Lisa's recollection? She was under the impression that Elizabeth Burton was the killer? That she has no knowledge of the two people Jill & Christian are refering too, as being the killers? Which was something Jill & Christian couldn't understand? That if it wasn't Lisa who sent them the text message, then who was it? Not a minute later? After the thought crosses their minds. Jill would receive another text message from this anonymous person. Telling her that" This is where things get interesting"? That had them all wondering what does that mean? As Lisa found it to be another break in the story that may have some value. That got Jill & Christian thinking about the witness Danny Burton was refering too? That knows about the things that went on throughout these murders? Which is another piece of the puzzle that remains a mystery? That needs to be identify as part of the missing link in the chain that needs to be solve?

Printed in the United States
By Bookmasters